CHARON'S QUEST

An Underworld Saga Novel

Eva Pohler

Published by Green Press

This book is a work of fiction. The characters, happenings, and dialogue came from the author's imagination and are not real.

CHARON'S QUEST. Copyright 2018 by Eva Pohler.

FIRST EDITION

Book Cover Design by Keri Knutson of Alchemy Cover Design.

Library of Congress Cataloging-in-Publication has been applied for

ISBN-13: 978-1983691355

ISBN-10: 1983691356

Chapter 1

"Off the boat," Hades demanded.

Charon looked up at his master, unsure if he'd heard him correctly.

"I've had a visit from Apollo." Hades crossed his arms and widened his stance. "Your future is unclear, but your demise is certain if you do not leave my kingdom."

"Leave, my lord?" Charon's bones were tired, and it pained him to speak.

"Haven't you noticed how aged and withered you've become? You're no good to me like this."

"I don't understand."

"My dear Charon, why are you the only one among us who has aged like an old man?"

Charon glanced at his trembling, bony hands and wrinkled, spotted flesh.

"Apollo saw the answer in a vision," Hades said. "Off the boat. Follow me."

Charon rarely left the skiff—only to sleep in his abode on the night of each full moon. When he did leave the boat, he flew, because to walk was painful.

He followed Hades down the winding corridor of the Underworld along the river of fire. He did not need the soft glow from the Phlegethon to see his master walking ahead of him, upright, muscled, virile. Unlike Hades, Charon's frail back was bowed—even in flight— and every bone trembled with old age.

So, he was to get his youth back, eh? Charon couldn't care less about it. And the last thing he wanted was to visit the Upperworld, where he hadn't

1

set foot since the beginning of time. Why did Apollo have to stir up trouble for him?

Hades rounded the corner and entered the foyer of his and his queen's main palace. "Have a seat."

Charon flew to one of the oversized wooden chairs gathered around a golden table. He couldn't recall ever sitting in this room before.

Hades paced across from him. "I'll allow you to retain your powers, as long as you don't abuse them. You'll need money...and better clothes. Perhaps a cane."

Charon's old robes were immediately replaced by dark gray trousers and a pale button-down shirt with long sleeves. His old rubber boots disappeared, and in in their place were short black boots made of leather. A black wooden cane appeared in his hand and a gray fedora on his head.

"That's better," Hades said.

This was all too much. Charon already missed his robes.

"I didn't think it possible for a god to die, my lord."

"You seem to be the exception, my friend." Hades continued to pace, and now he scratched his beard. "Apollo says it's because you vicariously experience the lives of each soul that boards your skiff."

Charon rubbed his temple, where a new pain was forming. While it was true that the lives of each soul flashed before his eyes, it hadn't occurred to him that his aging was the result.

"Might Apollo be mistaken?" Charon asked.

"I suppose there's a first time for everything," Hades replied. "Even so, we should err on the side of caution."

Charon bit his trembling lip.

Hades stopped pacing to study him. "I would think you'd be grateful for the chance to go out on adventures of your own, for a change. Why so glum?"

"Glum seems hardly the right adjective, my lord. Terrified is more like it."

Hades sat in the chair opposite him and furrowed his brow. "You forget who you are. Why should a god be terrified to go among mortals?"

"I'm a creature of habit. I like my life just as it is. I've never been anywhere but here, in your kingdom. This is my home. I prefer it to anyplace else."

Hades laughed and clapped him hard on the shoulder, nearly cracking his clavicle in half. "My dear Charon, it's not like you won't be coming back. Think of this as an opportunity to spread your wings."

"I haven't got wings, my lord."

"Metaphorically speaking."

Charon sighed, realizing there was no getting out of it. "What would you have me do?"

"That's more like it. Chin up! I'm truly happy for you to have this chance. You can travel the world, meet interesting people, and do exciting things."

Charon would rather have none of it.

Hades climbed to his feet and resumed his pacing and the scratching of his beard. "Where should I send you first? One of the great cities, perhaps?"

"I know little of the Upperworld, my lord. I've come to understand bits of it from the souls I ferry."

"And from those bits, aren't you curious about the world? Isn't there something you wonder about?"

There was one thing he wondered about. He never imagined he'd have the chance to experience it.

"The cinema," Charon said. "I wonder about the cinema."

The corners of Hades's mouth curled up into a gleeful smile. "Well, then. I know exactly where to send you, my old friend."

* * *

Charon emerged at night amidst a bustling city. Although he'd retained his godly powers, he didn't need night vision to see the automobiles crawling by on the streets, or the people walking briskly to who knew where. Nor did he need the starlight, invisible here beneath the smog. The ample light emanating from the signs, streetlamps, and headlights was more than enough to make everything about this crowded, dirty place visible.

He hobbled along with his cane and entered the cinema. While he'd retained his powers, Hades had warned him against using them. His lord had said that if mortals discovered they had a god among them, Charon would have no chance to enjoy his experience. The constant requests and complaints would sabotage his efforts at happiness.

The last thing Charon wanted was to be bothered by people.

He reached into his trouser pocket for one of the golden coins given to him by Hades and handed it to the clerk.

"Um, cash or credit card, sir," the boy said as he turned over the coin.

"The gold is more than enough for a ticket," Charon said, compelling the pimpled youth to cooperate, since there were no other mortals around to witness it.

"Which show, sir?"

"You choose."

4

"What genre do you like?" the boy asked. "Drama? Comedy? Suspense?"

Charon grinned. "I like it all."

The clerk handed over a ticket and Charon walked past.

The theater was half-empty when Charon entered and found a seat on the end of the first row, away from others. As the movie played, he forgot where and when he was as he ran the full gamut of emotions. He laughed, he cried, and he gasped in surprise, and he cried again at the end.

When the film ended, he used his cane and the arm of his seat to pull himself to his feet. Getting up was much more difficult than getting down. Among the others leaving the room, he plodded along, deciding to go to the room next door, where another film was about to begin. No one stopped him. He sat in the same row, same seat.

The comedy left him in a delightful mood. He decided to try one more film. The movie in the room next door had already begun. He found his seat and watched.

The third film left him feeling terrified. His hands were shaking—worse than usual—and he could barely breathe. Wasn't the purpose of coming to the Upperworld to restore his youth and vitality? And yet, he felt worse than ever.

As the others in the theater made their way to the exit and the lights turned on, Charon sat there, holding his chest. There was a new pain there—a tightness that left him crippled.

"Sir? Are you okay?" a woman asked him.

Before Charon could reply, Thanatos appeared beside the woman. Now that Charon was focused on regaining his youth, he was struck by the disparity between his shriveled, wrinkled flesh and the youthful vibrancy of Thanatos. His bright blue eyes shone down at him beneath wavy, dark hair. His complexion was flawless, his shoulders and chest broad and strong.

"Have you come for me?" Charon asked the youthful god.

"Excuse me?" the woman asked.

The woman couldn't see Death.

Thanatos frowned. "We need to talk. Come with me."

Taking him by the arm, Thanatos god-traveled with Charon from the cinema to a brightly-lit hotel room with two beds, a sofa, and a table and chairs.

"I just collected a soul from this room," Thanatos said. "The body is in the bathtub."

"Won't there be a stench?"

"You can book your own room downstairs," Thanatos said. "But first, we need to talk. Have a seat."

Charon eased himself into one of the two wooden chairs beside the table.

"When you said you liked the cinema, Hades thought you might enjoy a tour of Universal Studios," Thanatos said. "That's why he sent you here, to L.A."

"A tour?"

"To learn how the movies are made."

Charon waved his hand at the wrist. "I don't care about that. I only care about watching them."

"That's no different than seeing the lives of others flash before your eyes," Thanatos pointed out. "It won't help."

"Hmm."

Charon looked up at his old friend, comforted by his presence. They'd spent most of their time on the skiff together. Thanatos—or Than, as most of the

6

Underworld gods called him—brought the souls and remained aboard until the dead reached their final resting place—whether that was the Fields of Elysium for the good, Tartarus for the wicked, or Erebus for those needing time to heal. Charon had rarely exchanged words with him in the last century or two, because it pained him to speak; but it hadn't always been so.

"You need to experience life," Than said. "I envy you this chance. You need to take full advantage."

Charon chuckled.

"What's so funny?"

"The irony," Charon said. "Death telling me about life."

"If not a tour, then what?" Than asked.

"Take me somewhere," Charon said. "Be my guide."

"You know mortals can't tolerate me," Than replied.

"I'd forgotten. They drop dead in your presence."

"Not immediately, but still."

"I don't like people anyway," Charon said. "Take me someplace where I can have adventures away from others."

Thanatos grimaced. "That's rather missing the point, isn't it?"

"I disagree." Charon climbed to his feet, which wasn't easy. "Put me on a boat on a river somewhere. You have the remarkable ability to be everywhere at once. Come with me."

Than crossed his arms. "I'll make a deal with you."

"Now you sound like your father."

"I'll keep an eye on you, until you find a companion," Than said. "You'll need American money—not the gold my father gave you."

Than handed him a wallet made of leather. Charon opened it to find it stuffed with pieces of green paper.

"That's a magical wallet," Than said. "It won't run out of money and will supply you with the right currency for whatever country you happen to visit."

"What do I need it for?"

"Use it to buy things—like food and clothes. Don't wear the same trousers and shirt each day."

Charon rolled his eyes. "You want me to go shopping?"

"And meet someone," Than said.

"That'll be easy," Charon said sarcastically.

"Then I'll put you and him—or her—on a boat on a river of your choosing."

"How do you expect me to do that? It'll take time to get someone to trust me enough to go on a trip like that. Your deal is worthless."

Thanatos put a hand on Charon's shoulder. "This city is full of people. Surely you can make friends with one of them."

"I don't know where to start."

Thanatos turned away. "Try the bar downstairs."

* * *

Charon took the elevator to the first floor and found the bar across from the lobby. A group in their mid to late thirties sat together at one table, but, otherwise, the place was quiet with a couple in a corner booth and two individuals sitting at either end of the bar.

Charon hobbled across the room to sit on a stool at the center of the bar.

"What can I get for you, sir?" The bartender was a young woman in her twenties with long, black curls pinned behind her ears and a chocolate complexion with rosy cheeks.

Charon had only ever drunk ambrosia and the wine of Dionysus. "You choose."

The young woman smiled. "Are you thirsty for something sweet or sour? Something stiff or weak?"

"Something stiff and not sweet."

"You'll want a shot of whiskey then," she said. "Do you have a favorite brand?"

Charon shook his head. "Give me your finest."

The spunky bartender poured him a glass and set it before him.

She watched as he put the glass to his lips and tasted the whiskey.

"Mmm." Charon gave her a smile. "This will do."

"You look familiar," the bartender said. "I think I've seen you before."

Charon squinted at the inscription on her nametag. "That's unlikely, Matilda."

The bartender poured another drink and delivered it to the man at the far end of the bar. When she returned, she asked, "Are you from around here?"

"Nowhere near," he said before taking another sip of the smooth whiskey.

"I know I've seen you before," she said. "I bet I'll figure it out before the night's over."

Charon lifted his glass, as if to toast her. "You do that."

Matilda left to attend to the large group. When she returned, she said to Charon, "Enjoy the quiet while you can. It's about to get busy in here."

"What makes you say that?" he asked.

"The parade is nearly over."

Charon frowned. "Parade?"

"Dia de los Muertos. You must have passed it on your way here. It's been going on for three days."

"The Day of the Dead?" Charon had never heard of such a thing.

"I guess you *aren't* from around here." Matilda poured five drinks and then delivered them to the large group.

Charon now had a vague memory of having learned about the celebration from some of the souls who boarded his skiff. Halloween. Melinoe's night. Some of the dead who'd managed to escape Thanatos were rounded up and brought home. But the mortals believed the dead were released from their resting place and allowed to walk among them. Centuries ago, people disguised themselves out of fear, to blend in with the other ghosts. Somehow this tradition had become an elaborate, week-long festival, complete with music, art, dancing, costumes, and—according to Matilda—parades.

He wondered if it had been Apollo or Hades who'd decided to send Charon to the Upperworld during Dia de los Muertos. And, whoever it was, did he think he was being funny?

When Matilda returned behind the bar, she took a rectangular, flat device from her trouser pocket and held it to her ear. Although she spoke into it softly, Charon could hear her every word. He realized she was speaking to someone on a phone.

Matilda was being told that someone named Kayla didn't have much time to live, that Matilda needed to prepare herself and visit the hospital as soon as she was able.

The bartender wiped tears from her cheeks and returned the phone to her trouser pocket. When she noticed Charon's empty glass, she asked, "Ready for another?"

Charon gave her a nod and watched her fill his glass before bringing it to his lips. Matilda's dramatic change in mood unsettled him, so he said, "Death isn't so bad, you know."

She stopped mixing her next concoction and narrowed her eyes at him. "You sure have good ears for a person your age."

He shrugged. "What can I say? That's true."

He took another sip of the whiskey, enjoying the numbing effect it was having on his aches and pains.

The bartender continued mixing her drinks but said, "I'm not worried for Kayla. I know she's going to a good place. I'm worried for her parents and brother." Tears fell down the young woman's lovely face. "And I'm worried for me, because she was my friend."

Charon didn't know what to say. How could the loss of one person affect so many people?

"It may not seem like it now," he began. "But life will go on for the rest of you. I doubt you'll have any trouble making a new friend."

Matilda's face twisted into a deeper frown as more tears leaked from the corners of her eyes. Clearly, he'd said the wrong thing.

Just then the glass doors to the street swung open, and a crowd of people with painted faces and jeweled costumes burst into the bar, filling the remaining tables and booths. Their faces were painted white and resembled skulls. Some of the women wore black veils with short dresses, while others wore paper flowers in their hair and long, colorful skirts. One of the men wore a sombrero and a black suit, while others were dressed in ragged clothing decorated with fake blood.

11

Matilda sighed, wiped her cheeks, and went to take their orders.

Charon watched the mortals dressed in their depictions of death and couldn't help but laugh at them. They must be desperate for an excuse to have a party. Then he supposed one had to pass the time somehow, so why should he judge them?

When Matilda returned with an air of exhaustion, Charon leaned over the bar and said, "This might not mean much to you, but I thought you should know that you are the first real person with whom I've ever had a conversation." He laid down a handful of cash from the wallet Thanatos had given him. "Thank you."

Matilda stared at the money as her mouth dropped open in surprise. "That's over two hundred dollars, sir."

"You keep the change," Charon said.

She covered his hand with hers as more tears slipped down her cheeks. "Your kindness couldn't have come at a better time. Thanks so much."

Then he heard her unwitting prayer to him: *You are the kindest person I've ever met.*

Charon, like the other gods, couldn't read the thoughts of mortals; however, when a person directed a prayer to him personally, wittingly or not, he could hear it clearly. Not wanting to give away his godly status, he ignored it.

As he stood from the stool to leave, he found it easier to move. Apparently, speaking with someone had worked wonders on him. He wondered what good it would do to speak to a group. Maybe interacting with more people would multiply the effect.

He crossed over to the painted faces gathered around the tables and waved.

"I hope you enjoy your celebration," he called out.

"Join us, Senor!" the man in the sombrero said to him. "Pull up a chair and have a drink on me!"

Charon would rather return to the lobby, rent a room, and retire in solitude, but because he hoped to regain more of his strength and stamina from the encounter, he accepted the young man's offer. A chair was brought over from another table and scooted into the middle of the group, where Charon sat, despite his misgivings.

"What are you drinking?" the man with the sombrero asked. "Bartender, please bring this man another of whatever he's having."

Matilda brought him another whiskey, and it went down smooth.

"Thank you," Charon said to the man with the sombrero.

"De nada, Senor," the man said. "So, tell me, do you have any advice to give for how to live a long and fruitful life?"

Charon scratched his head beneath his fedora as the others in the group grew quiet and waited for his answer. "Avoid Death."

His new companions broke out in boisterous laughter.

"Claro que si!" The man in the sombrero stood up and held his glass aloft. "A toast! May we all avoid death as long as humanly possible!"

"Cheers!" one of the women shouted.

"Cheers! To avoiding death!" another said.

The group clinked their glasses together and drank to the toast. Charon felt himself feeling more energetic. For the first time in centuries, he straightened his back in his chair.

After a few more minutes, he stood to leave, thanking the man in the sombrero for the drink. He waved goodbye to Matilda and had already reached the lobby when she rushed to his side and said, "You forgot your cane."

"Thank you," he said, as he took it from her— though he no longer needed it. Then he added, "I hope you'll get to see your friend once more before she dies."

"It's too late," Matilda said, fighting sobs. "I just received word. She's gone."

A feeling quite foreign to Charon compelled him to comfort the poor mortal. He put his arms around her and cupped the back of her head with his hand.

"Not gone," he said. "Just not here. She's somewhere else."

Matilda collapsed against him, and he was surprised that he could hold her weight. She was petite, but, before tonight, he could barely manage his own weight, much less that of another. More of his strength had returned.

He'd never held a living being against him like this. Her beating heart pounded against his, and her warm flesh was a comfort to him, even though he meant to comfort *her*. She smelled lovely. He felt as if he could hold her there, in the middle of the lobby, for a very long time.

"Thank you," she said when she pulled away. But when she met his gaze, her brows furrowed into an expression of perplexity.

"What's wrong?" he asked.

"Nothing." She continued to stare up at him. "It's just that, in this light, you seem much younger than I thought you were."

Charon turned to look at his reflection in the mirrored wall behind the front desk of the lobby. He was fully upright and less thin—more robust. He had more hair on his head beneath his hat, though it remained gray. Instead of a man on his death bed, he looked like a respectable man in his sixties. He rather liked the change.

"You're the reason for it," Charon said, turning to Matilda. "You make me feel like a younger man."

Matilda blushed and smiled. "Goodnight, sir." She turned to leave.

"Goodnight." He watched as she retreated to her place behind the bar.

Now a new feeling penetrated his heart. The only word he could think of to describe this new feeling was *longing*.

Chapter 2

Although it hadn't been a full moon—which was the usual time when he slept—Charon had returned to his room and had dozed off out of boredom. When sunlight trickled in through the curtains, he was brought from his dreams sooner than he'd wished. He'd been holding the bartender Matilda in his arms and comforting her.

He climbed from the bed, still wearing his shirt and trousers, to find his clothes wrinkled. He put on his hat and boots and headed out to the street to shop for new ones.

The delicious smells on the corner led him to a bakery, where he had a roll and coffee before continuing his journey. He felt better than he had in centuries. The cool morning air was crisp and invigorating, and the smog no longer bothered him.

As he passed a store window, he was surprised to see Matilda inside the shop. Instead of her black trousers, black blouse, and white apron from last night, she wore a pretty sweater, short skirt, and tall boots. Her long curly hair was pinned back on each side, showing off her nice cheek bones, as it had the night before. She was standing in front of a row of greeting cards and was picking through them.

He entered the shop and watched her as she opened one card, read it, laughed, and replaced it. Then she opened another and did the same. Her laughter, her bright face, and her sweet smile made him smile, too.

He felt frumpy and embarrassed by his wrinkled clothes, so he didn't try to speak with her. He turned and headed back out to the street.

He walked the streets for another hour, peering into shop windows but never venturing into them. Once, he stopped to speak to a shopkeeper on the sidewalk about the price of trousers; otherwise, he kept to himself. How was he supposed to find a companion to sail along a river with him in this crowded city? He had nothing to offer a friend and nothing to talk about. These people scurrying in and out of shops had nothing in common with him. In fact, he was all but invisible to them.

Maybe he'd have to forget the idea of boating on a river. Maybe he'd have to find adventures among the masses. But what? What was there to do other than shop and eat and tour theme parks? He had no interest in museums. He knew enough about human history and its art and culture from the memories of the souls in Hades. Was there anything worthwhile to occupy his time?

He was thinking of Matilda when he saw her again as she entered the double glass doors of an enormous corner building. It was a hospital.

Charon decided to follow her. Was she ill? Or was she going to pay her respects to her friend who'd passed the day before?

He followed her from a safe distance up a stairwell to the second floor. When she turned a corner, he nearly lost her, until he heard someone greet her. He continued down the hall toward the sound of her voice and flattened against the wall, out of sight, when he saw her standing at what must be a nurses' station, where a woman was handing Matilda a garment—what Charon believed was called "scrubs."

"Johnny's been asking for you," the woman said to Matilda. "He'll be glad to see you again."

"Why?" Matilda's face darkened. "Is it almost time?"

The woman behind the desk shrugged. "It's hard to tell. You know how it is. Could be hours, could be months."

Matilda slipped the green garment over her head and pushed her arms through its sleeves before saying, "I don't know how the families can take it."

"It's hard for the doctors, too," the other woman said. "You'll find out soon enough."

"Not that soon. I've got two more years before I can even begin my residency." Matilda continued down the hall. She looked cute with her short skirt jetting out from beneath the green top.

The other woman called out, "It goes by faster than you think."

Charon followed Matilda through a set of double doors, over which a sign read "Children's Ward."

When she entered a room, he waited outside the door to eavesdrop.

"Hey, Johnny," Matilda said.

Charon was expecting to hear a child's voice, but it was the low voice of a young man that answered. "There you are, Beautiful."

Matilda laughed.

Was this a boyfriend?

"I brought you a card," she said. "Open it."

Charon heard the slight tear of paper. Then there was nothing but the sound of the mortals breathing, until the young man burst into laughter.

"That's the best one yet," Johnny said. "Thanks."

"I love to see you laugh," Matilda said. "You're pretty darn handsome when you do."

18

There was an awkward silence, until Johnny said, "How's school?"

"It's killing me."

Johnny laughed.

"I'm sorry," Matilda said. "That was insensitive."

"Oh, stop," Johnny protested. "You don't have to walk on egg shells around me."

"School wouldn't be so bad if I didn't have to work late, standing on my feet all night," Matilda added. "I need more sleep."

"You can sleep when you're dead," Johnny said.

"Stop it."

"What? You started it."

"True." Then she said. "Well, your vitals look great. And your coloring looks better than it did last week. How do you feel?"

"Better now that you're here."

She laughed. "So much cheese! Ugh!"

"What? Are you vegan or something?"

Matilda laughed again. "You're cray-cray."

"What are you? Ancient? No one says that anymore."

"Oh, stop teasing me."

"But it's so much fun." Then, Johnny added, "Will you come back by after your rounds?"

"Of course, I will," Matilda said. "I told you. You're my favorite."

"I bet you say that to everyone," Johnny teased.

Charon heard the sound of a kiss. Was it on the cheek? The forehead? The lips?

"Maybe I do," Matilda teased. "See you later."

Charon realized Matilda was on her way out of the room, but not in time to react. She saw him, standing there in the hallway.

"Oh, hello," she said, recognizing him. "Wow."

He wasn't sure how to take her comment. "Wow?"

"The light in the hotel does *not* do you justice, sir," Matilda said. "Beneath these florescent lights, you look much younger."

"I was tired last night."

"And I see you're without your cane."

"A temporary injury," he quickly explained. "It seems I'm healed."

"Are you here visiting someone?" she asked.

"No," he said, before realizing his mistake. "I mean, yes."

"Oh? Which patient? I know them all."

Charon swore to himself. "Um, not in this ward. In another. I thought I recognized you, so..."

Her smile left her face, and her eyes widened. "You followed me?"

He was at a loss. Why did she seem upset that he would follow her? "I mean you no harm."

"Is there something I can do for you?" The friendliness had left her voice, and now she was nothing but business-like. Her unwitting prayer to him was this: *I should have known your generous gift would come at a price.*

Charon tried to think quickly for some excuse that might be acceptable to this mortal woman. "I, I'm new to town, you see. Visiting a sick relative. And, when I saw you, I thought maybe you..."

"Yes?" She frowned.

"I thought maybe you might recommend a good restaurant for dinner," he finally said.

She seemed relieved. "What kind of food do you like?"

"Greek," he said.

"George's on South Figueroa," she said. "It's not far from the hotel."

He tipped his hat. "Thank you, Matilda."

"You're welcome, sir."

He turned and left, feeling relieved that things hadn't gone worse than they had. Nonetheless, the encounter had been somewhat of a disaster, and he realized more than ever how impossible Thanatos's task of finding a companion would be.

He left the hospital and headed in the direction of his hotel. On the corner of the next block, a black dog greeted him. The animal reminded Charon of Cerberus when he was a pup—except, of course, this animal had only one head. Charon stroked the dog behind its pointed ears.

"Hello, there," Charon said as he petted the dog. "What are you doing here in the big city?"

"Starving," the dog replied with a bark.

"I have no food," Charon said. "But I can get you some."

Charon looked down one side of the street and then the other, realizing he was hungry, too. Noticing a sign in Greek, he headed that way. The dog followed him. It wasn't George's, but it would have to do.

"Your dog isn't allowed in here," a worker inside the restaurant complained.

"He's not my animal," Charon said. Then to the dog he said, "Wait outside."

A few minutes later, Charon returned to the street with a chicken kabob. He fed half of it to the dog and ate half of it himself.

"You're very generous," the dog said. "No one's ever been this kind to me."

Standing there on the curb, Charon asked, "Where do you live? Alone here on the streets? Or do you have a family?"

"I live with a cruel master who beats and starves me," the dog said. "Last night, I barely escaped with my life."

"I'm sorry to hear that," Charon said.

"You're the first person to understand me," the dog said.

Charon laughed. "That's because I'm a god, but don't let on you know."

"Why are you here, in this city?" the dog asked. "I thought gods lived in heaven."

Two men in business suits walked passed, so Charon waited until they were out of earshot to continue speaking with the dog.

"My master, Hades, sent me here for adventures," Charon said in a low voice as he squatted near the ground to pet the dog. "So, I best be off. Good luck, my friend."

Charon turned away from the dog and continued down the street.

"Wait," the dog barked, following behind.

Charon turned.

"Take me with you," the dog said.

"I'm afraid that's not possible. Go on, now."

"Please!" the dog barked.

Charon rolled his eyes and turned to face the dog. What had he gotten himself into? Was this his reward for being nice? "Look, you need to go your way, and I'll go mine. You're free now. You can do anything."

"I want to go with *you*," the dog insisted.

"You don't know what you're asking," Charon said. "I'm leaving the city—for a while anyway. A boat is no place for an animal."

Charon turned and continued down the street, but he could sense the dog following him. He sighed and tried to ignore him.

He went a few more blocks, searching for a pub, where he might have a chance at striking up a conversation. When he turned a corner, he caught a glimpse of the dog still following a few yards behind him.

Charon stopped, turned, and frowned at the dog, who was now a few feet away. "What do you want from me?"

"A friend," the dog said. "I have none."

Charon paused and wiped his brow. He understood how it felt to be alone in the world. Maybe he should give the dog a chance to be a friend to him. The animal was certainly an improvement on the human race. "I can't promise you won't be sorry."

"I'll take my chances, if it's alright with you," the dog replied.

"Follow me," Charon said, hoping he wouldn't regret it.

The dog wagged his tail and trotted happily beside him as Charon made his way down the street, looking for a private place to summon Thanatos. Charon turned down an alleyway and prayed to the god of Death.

Moments later, Thanatos appeared.

"I've found my companion," Charon said.

Than looked at the animal.

"I want to go on adventures, too," the dog barked.

Than crossed his arms and cocked his head to one side. "This wasn't what I had in mind."

"You said to make a friend, and I did," the ferryman argued.

The dog licked Charon's hand.

"What's your name?" Than asked the dog.

"Bill," the animal replied.

Thanatos turned to Charon. "You're already anxious to abandon the city for your boat on a river?"

Charon thought of Matilda, but quickly realized he couldn't attract her attention in his current condition. To her, he was an old man.

"Yes," Charon said. "Put us on a river not far from here, where we can enjoy what this world has to offer without having to bother with people."

Than arched a brow. "Not far from here? Why?"

"No reason," Charon lied. He didn't want to go too far away from Matilda. But why? He barely knew her. "For the sake of convenience."

"Fine," Than agreed. "You'll need different clothes—blue jeans and work boots, and a jacket, too, I suppose."

Charon was pleased to get out of shopping when his pants and shirt were soon replaced with proper work clothes.

Bill barked his approval. "When do we go?"

Before Charon could reply, he found himself standing on a skiff—only slightly larger than his own—on a wide river. Bill stood in front of him at the bow, glancing around in surprise.

"What the what?" Bill barked. "How did we get here?"

"Thank Death," Charon replied.

Chapter 3

The temperature was decidedly cooler as Charon steered the boat in the narrow channel through a rock archway and out into a wide expanse of water. Bill didn't seem bothered by the chill in the air, as his tail wagged happily. On each bank, the trees and shrubs, still holding onto their leaves, were vibrant golds, oranges, and tans. The sky above was clear and breathtakingly beautiful. Charon had never seen it so blue.

"Tell me about your life," Charon said, missing his ability to see the lives of the souls entering the Underworld.

"There's not much to tell," Bill said from the bow, his tail no longer wagging. "It was all so confusing."

"What do you mean?"

A bird flew overhead, screeching a peculiar song, and they were momentarily distracted by it.

Then Bill said, "I was born in a cage and lived with my mother and brothers and sisters for a short while. I was happy enough, until my master came and took me to his house. My life went downhill from there."

"What happened?" Charon wanted the details.

Bill sat back on his haunches. "At first he was nice to me. I was terrified. I didn't want to leave my family, especially my mother." Bill swiped at a tear. "But he comforted me. That first day, he doted on me."

"What changed?"

"Like I said, it was all so confusing. I could never figure out what he expected of me. He was an emotional man. I soon put it together that he'd recently lost someone he loved. I think it was his wife. I think I made him happy, at first." Bill lay on his belly and rested his snout on the boat. "I wish that day hadn't ended."

"When did he begin to beat you?" Charon asked.

"That very first day," Bill said. "I didn't know where I should relieve myself, so I found a corner in his small townhome. I thought it was out of the way and was a good choice, but he felt differently."

"You were just a pup. How could you know?"

Bill nodded. "I tried another spot, and another."

"And nothing pleased him."

"Exactly." Bill stood up, circled around, and sat back down. "After a few days of this madness, I began to understand that he wanted me to do it in the small side-yard he shared with his neighbor."

"Did things improve for you then?"

"They would have if my master had let me out often enough. He'd fall asleep for hours and hours. He drank and passed out at all hours of the day. What was I to do?"

Charon could see Bill's predicament.

"And, worst of all, it was never clear to me what was mine and what was his."

"Why was that a problem?" Charon asked, noticing a group of butterflies scattering from one of the shrubs on the closest bank.

"He bought me toys, in those first few months. Even though he screamed at me, beat me, and, on one occasion, threw me across the room, he still had moments of kindness back then. He gave me ropes to tug on, squeaky toys to fetch, and cute little stuffed animals to rip apart. He left them scattered on the floor for me. One morning, I thought he'd given me his shoes, because he left them beside my toys on the floor. I was so excited, and I ripped one of them with pleasure. That's when he chained me to the stake in the side yard. He never let me into the house again."

"That hardly seems fair," Charon said. "It was your master's fault for leaving his shoes with your toys."

"He barely spent time with me after that. I lived for a very long time chained to the stake. My master brought me scraps to eat each evening, and I had a moldy bowl of water beneath a leaking faucet. I was forced to sit and lie down in my own waste. The only time he moved me was when it rained. I used to pray for rain, because I was then taken to the covered patio and tied to a post. It was a pleasant change from the nasty yard."

"No wonder you stink," Charon said.

"My master complained of that, too," Bill said, dropping his head with shame.

"I meant no offense, Bill," Charon quickly added, patting the dog on the head. "I don't mind it at all. And it's not your fault he never bathed you."

"There was no place to clean myself. To be honest, my smell offends even me."

"There's a simple solution to your problem," Charon said as he waved his hand toward the river.

"The river?" Bill cowered down and looked up at Charon with frightened eyes.

"Have you never been swimming?" Charon asked. It was the one thing Charon enjoyed as much as steering his boat. From time to time, he'd leap into the Acheron River and swim until he'd exhausted himself. Not often, but occasionally, Cerberus had been allowed to join him.

"I've never been anywhere but that nasty side yard," Bill explained. "Until today, when you found me after I'd escaped."

"Let's find someplace to dock." Charon directed the boat toward the nearest bank, which was still covered in brilliantly colored trees and shrubs. There was no sign of human life for miles. "This should do."

When the boat bumped against the shore, Charon climbed into the shallow water and pulled the skiff onto the grassy embankment.

Charon stripped from his clothes and tossed them into the boat. "From what I understand, dogs are natural swimmers."

The ferryman eased back into the cold water and waded out until he was chest deep.

"Come on, Bill!" Charon called.

He watched as the dog screwed up his courage.

"It's okay, boy!" Charon reassured him. "You can do it!"

Bill wagged his tail and flung himself into the water. When he emerged, he was shivering and struggling to stay afloat.

"Paddle to me," Charon said. "Just a few more yards."

Bill kept his gaze fixed on Charon as he struggled toward him in the water with a determined look on his face.

"Almost!" Charon cheered him on. "You're nearly here!"

When Bill was about two feet away, Charon reached out his arms and scooped the dog into an embrace. "You did it! Good boy, Bill!"

Bill wagged his tail eagerly, but he was as cold to the touch as the water, and he was shivering, his teeth chattering.

"Poor boy," Charon cooed, holding the dog close to his chest as he returned to the bank. "Let's get you warm and dry as soon as possible."

The ferryman stepped into his trousers and then used his jacket to dry the dog as best he could. Bill continued to shiver, so Charon held him close, using his body heat to warm him.

"I shouldn't have suggested it," Charon said regretfully. "I'd forgotten how intolerant mortals are of extreme temperatures."

"It was fun," Bill chirped through chattering teeth. "And I learned how to swim."

Charon rubbed the dog's wet coat, trying to create more heat. "Indeed. You should be proud."

When the dog continued to shiver despite Charon's efforts to warm him, Charon had an idea. Hemera, his sister and the goddess of daytime, whom he hadn't seen for centuries, might be able to help. He wrapped Bill tightly in the jacket and left him in the back of the boat. Then he stood up and called out for his sister.

She appeared before him in a halo of sunshine. "Why, I can't believe my eyes!"

"It's good to see you, too," Charon said.

"How did you escape your prison?" she asked.

Charon shook his head. "How many times have I told you and Aether that I love my job? The Underworld is my home."

"It's hard to believe that the three of us were cut from the same cloth—Aether being the upper air and I being daylight. How can you possibly be happy where the sun never shines?"

"You forget who our parents are," Charon said dryly.

"I never forget that," she said less cheerfully.

"I called you here because I need your help," Charon said.

Hemera crossed her arms and frowned. "I should have known it wasn't to be reunited with me. Charon! We haven't seen each other for ages!"

"I would have eventually come to see you, Sister," he said. "But I wanted to be in better form first."

"You look fabulous. What do you mean? You look much better than you did the last time I saw you."

He explained what Apollo had seen—why Charon had aged while the other gods had maintained their youth.

"Oh, I see," she said. "Well you look beautiful already. Distinguished even."

"Is that another way of saying I still look old?" Charon teased.

"What do you need from me, Brother?" Hemera asked, avoiding his question.

"Can you ask Helios to shine brightly on my dog? He's freezing, and I can't seem to warm him."

"Oh, you sweet thing!" Hemera said, embracing the animal that had been lying in the back of the boat. "I didn't see you there in the folds of my brother's coat."

Hemera lifted her arm into the sky and reached all the way up to where the sun god sat in his golden cup, flying across the clouds. Then she drew her arm back in to its original size as she cupped a flame in her hand.

"This should warm you," she said to the dog.

In a few moments, the dog's fur was dry.

"I can't thank you enough," Bill barked. "I feel much better. Clean and warm."

"You smell better, but not good," Charon said. "More like a river rat than a sewer, and that's progress, I suppose."

"Charon!" Hemera scolded.

"He's right," Bill said. "At least it's an improvement."

"You should take him down the Mississippi to La Crosse, to a hotel, and give him a proper bath," Hemera suggested, handing Bill over to Charon. "You both look like you could use a good meal as well."

"What do you say, Bill?" Charon asked the dog.

Bill barked his approval and wagged his tail.

"Hurry, because our mother will be coming to shoo me away, and Helios is already ahead of me, on his way to the other side of the world," Hemera added.

"Who's your mother?" Bill barked.

"Night," Charon said. "Also known as Nyx."

"Don't you want to see her?" Bill asked. "If I had a chance, I'd want to see my mother."

Charon scratched Bill behind the ears. "My mother isn't accessible anymore."

"Anymore?" Bill repeated.

"She once lived in Tartarus, in the Underworld, my home."

"As did I," Hemera explained. "And even then, we never saw each other. As soon as I flew home to Tartarus, she left to roam the Upperworld with our father. And when she came home, I took my leave. We never got along."

"She likes to have her way," Charon added. "That's why Hades made her leave Tartarus and take residence in a cave in the far east."

"Made her? I thought we escaped," Hemera said.

"I suppose it depends on who's telling the story," Charon conceded.

"It's much better this way," Hemera said. "I follow Helios, and Mother follows Selene, and their dwellings are close to ours."

"What about your father?" Bill asked.

Charon shook his head. "That's why our mother is so hard to get along with. She's either sleeping in her cave, or embracing our father, Erebus, as they fly around the world."

"I see what you meant by inaccessible," Bill laughed. "It's a wonder you don't have more brothers and sisters."

Charon chuckled and pet Bill behind the ears.

"Here comes Dusk," Hemera warned. "Better hurry." She waved. "It was good to see you."

"Likewise," Charon said. "And thanks again for your help."

As his sister flew away, Charon helped Bill into the boat and shoved off from the bank.

Charon jumped into the back of the boat as they headed south. "Now we need to get to La Crosse before nightfall."

"I thought you could see in the dark," Bill pointed out.

"I can. But the nighttime temperature this far north will be hard on you. Better to get you indoors at night until we're further south."

Bill ducked his head in shame. "I'm sorry to be a burden to you."

"Are you kidding me?" Charon laughed. "You're the best part of this trip! I'd be miserable without you."

Bill skipped up to the bow and wagged his tail with excitement, and both passengers smiled as they floated down the Mississippi beneath the falling dusk.

Chapter 4

Charon boarded the boat at a dock in La Crosse and, after being turned away from three hotels, found a little inn that was friendly to dogs not too far from the harbor. It was a good, thing, too, because he'd been about to use his godly powers to compel the innkeeper to accept Bill, even though it risked exposing what Charon was.

Once in the room, he drew a warm bath and filled it with soap that smelled like rosemary and lemon. Then he helped Bill into the tub, where he scrubbed the dog's coat.

"This must be what heaven feels like," Bill chirped.

"What's wrong with your ears?" Charon asked, noticing the way Bill kept scratching at them.

"They always itch," Bill said. "And after being in the river, they itch even more."

"On the outside or the inside?"

"The inside," Bill said. "Deep down, where I can't reach."

"That's no good," Charon said. "We need to find out why."

"Whoa," Bill said, cowering down in the tub. "You're not taking me to the vet, are you? Because the one and only time I went, I got my manhood taken away from me."

"You mean your doghood, don't you?" Charon said with a smile.

"Manhood. There's no better word."

Charon laughed. "I don't know any vets, so I'll have to pray to Apollo. He got me into this mess. Hopefully, he'll be amenable."

After Bill had been towel dried, Charon drained the tub and took a shower, enjoying the feel of the warm rain on his back. As he washed, he prayed to Apollo, asking him to relieve the problem with Bill's ears.

Charon hadn't finished drying himself off when Apollo, as golden as the sun, appeared in the next room holding a vial. Envious of his youthful appearance, golden-brown hair, and striking blue eyes, Charon was reminded of why everyone called Apollo the most beautiful god.

"Amazing," Apollo said upon seeing Charon. "What a remarkable improvement already."

"Thank you. I'm feeling much better."

"Not so resentful of me anymore, I see."

Charon smiled. "Not anymore. You were right. This was just what I needed. I've even made a new friend."

Bill barked his greeting.

"Hello," Apollo said to Bill.

"Is that vial for him?" Charon asked.

"Put a few drops of this solution in each of his ears once or twice a week, to keep the inner ear dry."

Apollo moved closer to Charon and cupped his cheek in his hand. "I'd forgotten how beautiful you once were. It's good to see you looking more like yourself again."

Charon blushed but said nothing.

Apollo placed the vial on the dresser and disappeared.

Charon wrapped himself in the clean, white, fluffy robe before taking the vial from the dresser and inspecting it. Bill wasn't too keen about the idea, but he cooperated as best he could while Charon applied the medicine to each ear.

"That feels funny," Bill said. "But thank you. No one's ever been this kind to me."

Charon patted the dog's head and scratched his back. "Likewise, my friend."

Bill wagged his tail. "Now, where can we get some food at this joint? I'm starving."

Charon noticed a menu sitting on the dresser across from the bed. He recalled many good memories from souls that had ordered room service in fancy hotels. "Shall we order something to be brought up?"

Bill jumped on the bed, ran in circles, and then stopped and wagged his tail.

"I'll take that as a yes," Charon said, laughing.

They shared a platter of steak and potatoes while they watched a movie. The movie made them laugh, and Bill rolled around the bed in delight after a few of the more hilarious scenes about an out-of-control but lovable dog bringing both chaos and happiness to a posh family. Charon was grateful for Bill's company and couldn't recall a day when he'd felt so much joy.

Worried that watching a movie would cause him to age again, Charon got up when the show ended to check his reflection in the bathroom mirror. To his astonishment, he looked ten years younger. His hair was less gray, showing more of the original brown wavy hair from his youth, and his skin was more vibrant. His eyebrows were darker, too, and thicker, making his brown eyes more youthful. He appeared like a man in his forties.

But why hadn't watching a movie aged him as it had before?

When he glanced back at the bed, he saw Bill curled on his side, snoring. Just the sight of the dog brought warmth to Charon's heart. Perhaps he hadn't aged during the movie because he had shared the experience with another. Maybe the key to his youth had more to do with connecting with others and sharing experiences than with anything else.

Charon returned to the bed and turned off the television, not wanting to make the mistake of watching more of it while his friend was asleep. He also turned off the lights and settled into the covers, since there was nothing else to do. Just as he closed his eyes to sleep, he felt his friend nuzzle up against him.

Charon felt the warmth of the animal against his back, and he felt his little heart pumping, too. He rolled over and curled the dog in the crook of his arm. Peace and joy washed over him, and, for the first time in his life, he realized what he'd been missing.

* * *

The following day, Charon and Bill floated together down the Mississippi River. The sun was bright in a blue sky, and the wind was cool but gentle. They were entertained by fish leaping in front of the boat along the way—at least, Bill was entertained by them. Charon took more enjoyment in Bill's reaction to the fish.

"There's another!" Bill barked, wagging his tail.

"Don't be a coward." Charon laughed with amusement. "Jump in after them. You know you want to."

"Only if you promise to call your pretty sister and have her dry my fur."

"You liked her, did you?"

"What was not to like?"

Charon laughed again. "If you want to catch a fish so badly, why don't we buy fishing poles and bait in the next town?"

Bill leapt so high into the air with glee that, for a moment, Charon worried the dog would fall overboard.

When Bill landed safely on the edge of the boat, Charon scooped him up in his arms and warned, "Mind yourself, boy. Unless you really do mean to jump overboard."

At that moment, a streak of lightning cut through the sky and struck the river less than a half a mile away. In the next instant, thunder roared overhead. Bill trembled in Charon's arms as a huge wave lifted them into the air. Above them, the face of Zeus appeared through a cloud.

His sharp blue eyes and ruddy cheeks were framed by reddish brown hair and a curly beard. The youngest of his siblings, Zeus was also the most powerful. Charon wondered why the king of the Olympians had taken notice of him.

"Hello, Charon," Zeus said.

With the boat perched on the wave high in the air, the Mississippi now far below them, Charon looked up at the king of the Olympians with fear. "Lord Zeus?"

"When Poseidon told me that he sensed you on his waters, I had to see for myself," Zeus explained. "Are you spying for Hades?"

Charon was taken aback. "Spying? No, my lord."

"Then explain to me why you aren't at your usual post."

The ferryman told the king about Apollo's vision and of Hades's orders to go on a quest for adventure. Meanwhile, Bill continued to tremble in Charon's arms, ducking his head into Charon's armpit.

Then the wave of water flattened, so quickly that, for many frightening moments, the skiff was suspended in thin air before it landed again on water and leveled out on the surface of the Mississippi. Charon clutched the dog close, feeling responsible for his wellbeing. They had barely managed to settle back to normal when Zeus appeared at the stern of the ship, the size of a mortal, not much larger than Charon.

"I have a proposition for you," Zeus said. "I want you to consider it carefully before you reply."

"A proposition, my lord?" Charon asked, not feeling very good about it.

"Yes. I want to grant you a wish in exchange for a favor."

"What favor, my king?" Charon asked.

"I want the helm of invisibility."

Charon's breath caught. For a moment, he stared back at Zeus, speechless.

"I see I've caught you off guard," Zeus said. "It's a compliment to you and to your master that you don't take such things lightly."

"I don't know what to say, my lord," Charon stuttered.

"I've wanted to get my hands on the helm for centuries," Zeus said. "Of all the gifts given to my brothers and me from the Fates, you might think my lightning bolt or Poseidon's trident the most useful."

Charon continued to gaze at the king of the gods.

"The truth of the matter is," Zeus continued, "the helm is the best of the three. I wish it had been given to me. I'm the one who saved my brothers and sisters from our father's belly. I should have been given the choice."

Charon supposed the Fates would not agree, but he was smart enough to keep his opinion to himself. Besides, he would never betray Hades.

"If you want the helm," Charon said, "you'll have to find another way to get it, my lord. I can't deceive my master. I don't have it in me."

Zeus clenched his jaw, and his face flushed. "Take some time to consider the matter."

"I don't need time, my king," Charon said.

Another streak of lightning sliced through the sky and struck the river. Zeus left the skiff just as the bow of the boat lifted onto the crest of another enormous wave and nearly capsized them.

Charon prayed to both Hades and Poseidon for help, since he, alone, was no match for the mighty Zeus.

But no help came.

The winds railed against them, tossing them this way and that. Charon prayed, not losing faith in his master.

But no help came.

In spite of Charon's efforts to keep it afloat, the boat capsized, and he and Bill plunged into the cold, dark river. During the fall, Charon lost hold of the dog, and as he now scrambled against river reeds, he lost sight of him, too.

"Bill!" Charon cried out through the cold, dark water. "Where are you, boy?"

Not finding him below, Charon fought the reeds and returned to the surface to scan the river in all directions for some sign of Bill. The boat, still overturned, floated away from him. Charon used his godly speed to catch up to it, where he checked beneath it for his friend. Not finding him there, he prayed again to Poseidon.

A river nymph with dark, golden skin from the waist up and silver scales and a tail from the waist down suddenly emerged from the water beside Charon as he was turning over the skiff to right it on the river. Her long dark hair, as dark as the Mississippi, clung to her body, hiding her feminine parts.

"Lord Poseidon couldn't come, so he sent me," she said.

"Thank you," Charon said. "I can't find my dog. I'm afraid he's drowned."

"There!" The river nymph pointed down river, where Bill was struggling to keep afloat as the current carried him away.

Charon and the nymph god-traveled to Bill and pulled him from the water.

"Thank Poseidon you're alive!" Charon cried as the nymph followed him back to the skiff, where he held Bill's limp and panting body in his arms.

Bill closed his eyes, struggling to breathe. Then he coughed up river water.

Charon gasped when he noticed blood trickling from the dog's mouth and ears.

"I'm afraid he's not out of the woods yet," the nymph said. "Better call Apollo."

Charon closed his eyes and prayed hard to Apollo.

When he appeared, the god of music and healing said, "You're making me regret informing Hades of my vision. You can't keep calling on me like this."

"Can you save him?" Charon asked.

Apollo looked over the dog. Then he put a hand on Bill's head. "He seems to have suffered a contusion to the brain. He's bleeding internally."

"But can you save him?" Charon asked again.

Thanatos appeared. "I'm afraid it's too late for that."

Tears rushed from Charon's eyes as he held the dog close. "It can't be. It *can't* be!"

With his eyes half closed, Bill looked up at him. He couldn't speak, but Charon could hear his prayer. Bill told him that he was the best friend he'd ever had, and he thanked the ferryman.

The dog's eyes rolled to the back of his head, and his tongue hung limply from his mouth.

Full of grief and desperation, Charon turned to Thanatos. "Isn't there something you can do?"

"If you only knew how many times that question is asked of me every day, my friend," Than said. "The answer is always the same. You, of all people, should know that."

Charon had never before felt the devastation he now realized was experienced at one time or another by every mortal who walked the earth. It made him feel sorry for them, for all the pain they endured when they lost someone they loved. He'd had a sense of it, from reading their memories as they boarded his skiff; but, before now, he'd never completely understood it, deep in his heart, like a wound that might never heal.

Zeus had done this to him for refusing to steal the helm. Charon knew better than to curse the king of the Olympians, but it took every bit of self-control not to.

"What will I do now?" Charon muttered bitterly. When no one replied, he said, "Take me home. I want to go back to Hades."

"I'm afraid you're not ready for that," Apollo said. "You must soldier on, my friend."

Apollo disappeared.

The river nymph took Charon's hand and said, "I'm sorry for your loss." Then she vanished into the river.

Thanatos clapped Charon on the back before squeezing his shoulder. "Maybe now that you know something of the human experience, you can tolerate their presence a little better."

Charon stroked Bill's fur and said, "I wouldn't go that far."

"Perhaps instead of avoiding mortals, you might use your time here to help them in some way."

"How?" Charon asked.

Than smiled. "Maybe that medical-student-slash-bartender can give you an idea."

Chapter 5

After he'd buried his friend along the bank of the Mississippi River beneath a cluster of pine trees, Charon had abandoned his skiff and had god-traveled back to Los Angeles, to the hotel where he'd first met Matilda. He secured a room for himself before hitting the streets, determined to buy something fine to wear. He felt more confident now that he looked like a man in his thirties—robust, virile, strong. He was still too old-looking to impress the likes of Matilda, but he wouldn't be forever.

A young clerk in a men's shop helped Charon find trousers and shirts in the style of the times. The trousers were made of a material called denim and were casually referred to as jeans. They fit him snugly, but the clerk said that was how they were supposed to look. As Charon checked in a full-length mirror to better see how the jeans fit him, he was pleased to see fuller limbs and muscles more befitting of a god. He should have always looked this way, he thought. He had every right to be as handsome as Thanatos and Hades and the others.

Once he'd paid for his new clothing and shoes, Charon walked down the street toward the hotel in search of the Greek restaurant Matilda had recommended. He was surprised by the unexpected attention he received from the ladies that passed him. If he'd still had his fedora, he might have tipped his hat to them.

Who was he kidding? He wouldn't have been so bold.

It wasn't long before he came upon George's on South Figueroa. He ordered a chicken kabob, rice, and vegetables. The kabob reminded him of the first day he'd met Bill. Full of longing and loneliness, he sobbed quietly over his meal.

It was evening when he walked back to the hotel and into the bar, hoping to find Matilda. There she was in her black blouse, black trousers, and white apron, mixing drinks. She didn't see him until he was standing in front of her with only the bar between them.

"What can I get you, sir?" she asked.

"Shot of whiskey, please." He rubbed his eyes, not wanting to show his sadness out in public.

"Do you have a favorite brand?" she asked.

She clearly hadn't recognized him. "Your finest, please."

"Are you alright, sir?" Matilda asked as she poured his drink.

"I will be," he said as he climbed onto the bar stool. "I recently lost someone very close to me."

She handed him the shot. "I'm sorry to hear that. I know how you feel. A friend of mine passed away a few days ago."

"My condolences."

She studied his face and frowned.

"Is something wrong?" he asked.

"Not at all," she said. "It's just that...well, by any chance, are you staying here with your father?"

It was Charon's turn to frown. "Why do you ask?"

"There was an older man here the other night. He was the kindest person I've ever met. Anyway, he resembled you. He walked with a cane and wore a fedora. I didn't catch his name. Any relation?"

Charon dipped his head to hide his embarrassment as blood flooded his cheeks. What

44

should he say? Should he lie? He couldn't very well tell her the truth without giving away his identity.

But before he could reply, she covered his hand with hers. Her touch ignited him. He felt about to burst into flames.

"I'm so sorry, sir. I don't mean to pry. But please tell me the person you lost wasn't your father."

"He was," he lied, to cover his identity. "His name was Bill."

Tears trickled down his cheeks. He hated feeling vulnerable, but her touch had overwhelmed him with so many emotions. She'd opened the floodgates, and he seemed unable to close them. He threw the whiskey back against his throat and swallowed the whole shot down at once.

She poured him another and said, "This one's on me."

He thanked her, noticing tears in her eyes. He was moved by her concern, even if it was only pity for an old man.

"I want you to know that one of his last acts was pure kindness," Matilda said gently. "He left me a generous tip—nearly two hundred dollars. It couldn't have come at a better time."

"I'm glad he helped you," Charon said.

Matilda left to take the order of a small party who'd just entered the bar and had sat at a table near the lobby. When she returned, she busied herself with mixing drinks as Charon sipped at his whiskey. She left to serve the new party, and when she returned, she refilled Charon's glass without asking if he needed more.

"Thank you, Matilda," he said.

"You're welcome, Mr....?"

"Just call me Charon."

She lifted her chin. "What an interesting name for a man."

"It's not a common one here? It is in Greece."

"It's common here for women—though if it's a Greek name, I doubt you spell it the same: K-A-R-E-N."

"C-H-A-R-O-N," he said. "And it's pronounced KAIR-uhn, not KAIR-*in*."

"Like the ferryman," she said.

"Exactly."

Matilda's face turned bright red.

"What is it, Matilda?" Charon asked.

"Excuse me," she said. Then she dashed off to check on the couple at the end of the bar.

When she returned, and as she began to mix drinks, Charon said, "My father left me a great deal of money, and I'd like to use it to help humanity in some way, but I don't know how. Any suggestions?"

As she met his gaze, her mouth dropped open. "Are you serious?"

"Very."

"I know exactly how you can help," she said. "Would you be willing to talk about an idea, either tonight after my shift ends or tomorrow afternoon?"

Charon felt a chill of pleasure crawl up his spine. "I'd be happy to meet you any time you'd like."

"I'm off in an hour, if you're willing to hang around. I can give you the details then, okay?"

Charon was filled with excitement and anticipation as he smiled and said, "I'll be here."

* * *

An hour and a half later, Charon and Matilda sat across from one another at a coffee and sandwich shop on the corner. Matilda had said she was starving and had invited Charon to join her. The little shop had no other patrons at this time of night, so they had the small, well-lit café to themselves.

Charon sipped a cup of coffee as Matilda cut her sandwich into bite-size pieces. In between bites, she told him things he already knew: that she was studying to become a doctor, that she volunteered in the children's ward, and that it was her mission to make the lives of the terminally ill children as pleasant as possible.

Matilda also told him some things he did not know: that her mother, a single parent, had died of cancer five years earlier and that her father had left them when she was still a baby. Although her parents hadn't married, Matilda had been given her father's name—Whitmore—and had considered tracking him down. When Charon asked why she hadn't yet, she said she wasn't sure she wanted to meet the man who'd abandoned her and her mother to a life of poverty. Matilda said she was making something of herself and was afraid he'd only welcome her into his life to leech off her hard work.

"I see," Charon said.

"I don't think it's in the cards anyway," she said.

"Why not?"

She wiped her mouth with a napkin. "Every time I've thought about searching for him, I've done a tarot reading, and, so far, a reunion hasn't looked good."

Charon lifted his brows. "You're a fortuneteller?"

Matilda laughed. "Sort of." She pulled a deck of cards from her purse. "Want a reading? It could be fun."

Charon shrugged. "Why not?"

Matilda shuffled the cards three times with her eyes closed. Then she held out the deck and looked up at him. "Cut?"

He'd seen enough memories to know what to do.

After he cut the cards, Matilda laid four out, face up, facing her. Her expression changed from curious, to bewildered, to troubled.

Charon frowned. "What do you see?"

She looked at him and blinked.

"Tell me," he said. "And be honest, no matter how dire my future may seem."

She pointed to the first card. "This sigil indicates that you will soon have to face a difficult decision."

"That seems rather broad. Couldn't it be whether to have sugar or cream in my coffee?—a difficult decision for me, since I don't drink the stuff often." In fact, he'd never had it before leaving the Underworld, and now he thought that, if he was to take anything back with him, it just might be coffee.

Matilda shook her head. "If you don't want the reading, I'll just put the cards away."

As she reached out to collect the cards, he stopped her with his hand. The warmth of her skin sent a jolt of fire up his arm to somewhere deep in his belly. "I'm sorry. Please keep going."

She glanced at him with a look of hesitation and reluctance. Her unwitting prayer was: *I don't usually reveal bad news.*

"Please," he insisted.

She sighed. "To be honest, I'm not sure what this spread is trying to tell me. It's very odd."

"In what way?"

"Well, the most obvious meaning is that you will be forced to make a difficult decision that will result in an important sacrifice."

"Sacrifice?"

She pointed to the second card in the spread. "Something heavy. Something life-changing."

He narrowed his eyes and studied her face. Did she really have the power to see the future?

Matilda pointed to the third card. "This sigil usually means death—not always literal, so don't freak out."

"You see my death?" Apollo had seen Charon's death, too. The quest for adventure was supposed to alter that fate, however. Maybe Apollo had been wrong.

"You told me to be honest," she said. "And it doesn't necessarily mean a *literal* death."

"What other kind of death is there?" Charon asked.

"Maybe this spread is referring to the death of your father," she said, unconvincingly. "Or maybe it means you lose some part of yourself, or become someone else entirely. I don't really know."

"Decision, sacrifice, death," he said.

"That's the most obvious interpretation," she said. "But this final card," she pointed to the fourth and final card in her spread. "This sigil is a reflection card that adds extra meaning to the others. It's strange because it also represents death. This has never happened to me in all the years I've been reading from this deck. Usually the death reflection card means that the experience represented in the spread will lead to your death, but how can death lead to death? The cards seem to be saying that you'll die twice."

"A death, a resurrection, and a final death," Charon said.

"Exactly." She met his gaze and held it for a few stunned moments before whispering, "Do you believe a person can come back from the dead?"

"It's rare but possible," he said.

She sat forward in her seat and smiled eagerly. "I'm so glad to hear you say that, because I believe it, too."

He studied her beautiful features—dark, round eyes, high cheek bones, thick lips. Her smile seemed to be an invitation. He wanted to lean over the table to touch his lips to hers, but he knew he must still be too old-looking in her eyes.

Her face seemed to light up as she said, "I'm going to tell you something, but don't freak out, okay?"

Her smile was contagious. "Okay."

She bit her lip. "Oh, never mind. You'll think I'm crazy."

"I could never think that of you."

"You don't even know me," she said as she waved a hand through the air in a dismissive way. "You can't know that. Maybe I *am* crazy."

"I'm no fortuneteller," he said, "but I can get a sense of a person."

"Oh?" she arched a brow. "And what is your sense of me?"

"You're kind, intelligent, and far from crazy."

"I might be a *little bit* crazy," she said with a laugh. "At least, you'll think so when I tell you the thing I'm hesitant to say."

"Spit it out."

"What if it ruins everything?"

"Ruins what?" Charon was baffled. What was there to ruin?

"Well," her blush deepened, "our friendship." Then her prayer was: *Can't you tell I'm interested in you?*

He was both moved and surprised. "I don't think you'll ruin anything." Then he added, "It's not in the cards."

She laughed. "I still haven't told you my idea for how you can help humanity."

"I knew we would eventually come to that."

"Have you ever heard of the Make A Wish Foundation?"

He searched the memories he'd seen, as the term sounded vaguely familiar, but came up with nothing.

"Anyway, it's this charity that grants wishes to terminally ill children," she said. "Like to go to Disney World, or to meet a famous person, or to see the Egyptian pyramids—you know, things like that."

"You want me to give my money to this charity?" he asked, understanding better where she was headed.

"Not just your money, necessarily."

He waited for her to explain.

"There's this sixteen-year-old boy at the hospital who doesn't have much time."

"Johnny?" he asked.

Her eyes widened. "How did you know?"

Charon cursed himself before saying, "My father mentioned him. He overheard you talking to him at the hospital."

Matilda smiled. "Of course. That makes sense. Anyway, Johnny has a bucket list, like we all do, I guess."

"A bucket list?"

"You know: dreams, wishes. Things he wants to do before he dies."

The waitress came and cleared away the empty plates before handing over the check. Charon insisted on paying it.

"I can explain the rest as we walk back," she said. "I have an early morning class and should get to bed soon."

"Do you live nearby?" Charon asked.

"In the hotel. I negotiated a free studio apartment as part of my contract. Should we head back?"

He helped her into her jacket and then, after she slung her purse over her shoulder, they left the café and walked in the cold night toward the hotel less than a block away. As they walked, Matilda told him more about Johnny.

"The Make A Wish Foundation will only grant one wish—not six—and so since Johnny can't choose the most important thing on his list, he hasn't put in for one."

"That's not very bright of him."

"Well, he's an orphan, and he has no family that could take him, so he doesn't think he has a chance, anyway."

"Oh, I see," Charon said. He realized now what Matilda had in mind. "Why can't *you* take him?"

She laughed. "I wish I could, but with work and school, I can't get away. Look, if you don't feel comfortable, you could just give money. That would be amazing all by itself."

"I'll take him wherever he wants to go," Charon said. "What's on his bucket list?"

Matilda gave him a coy smile, like she could sense he wanted to please her. "I volunteer tomorrow after my classes. Want to meet me at the hospital around four o'clock?"

They reached the hotel, so he opened the lobby door for her and followed her in. "I can do that."

"Great! I'm so excited!" she beamed.

As they waited for the elevator, with a few other patrons, he asked, "So what was it you wanted to tell me earlier, that you thought might ruin everything?"

She put her finger to her lips, which he understood to mean she couldn't say in front of the others. They rode the elevator to the fourth floor. He followed her to her room.

She unlocked the door with her key card and said, "Come in for a second, and I'll explain. But after that, I need to hit the sack."

He went to follow her inside but felt something preventing him from entering—like an invisible wall. He looked up and saw a symbol, like those on the tarot cards, scratched out on the upper frame of the door. He realized it must be a ward. But why would it affect him?

Embarrassed, he said, "It's late. Why don't you tell me tomorrow?"

Matilda frowned. "I'm surprised you aren't more curious."

He was incredibly curious, especially now that he realized she did more than read cards. If she used a protective ward over her door, she must be a witch.

"I want you to get your rest," he said. "Your rest is more important than my curiosity."

"What a gentleman," she said with a smile. "Okay then. See you tomorrow."

"Good night, Matilda."

As he turned to leave, he heard her unwitting prayer: *My, my, my, do you have one fine ass.*

Charon couldn't stop chuckling as he took the elevator to the seventh floor and returned to his room.

53

As he changed from his clothes, he caught his reflection in the bathroom mirror and was astonished to find he now appeared like a man in his late twenties—much more suitable for the likes of Matilda. This thought invigorated him, and, as he waited out the night, he found he could do nothing but daydream of her.

Chapter 6

The hospital was brightly lit, with colorful floor tiles and flowers at every turn, but the people wore expressions that dimmed the halls and made the place feel dark, as Charon found his way to the elevator and to the second floor. Even here, in the children's ward, the aroma of pine and disinfectant couldn't mask the other smells of urine and blood.

The sight of Matilda waiting for him outside Johnny's room brightened Charon's mood at once. Today she wore tight-fitting jeans that showed off her figure, in spite of the green smock she wore over her shirt as a volunteer. He felt a fire burning deep in his belly that made him tremble, like he had when he was old and couldn't control his muscles. But this feeling was different. It was exhilarating.

"Hi, Charon!" Matilda beamed up at him as he joined her in the hallway.

"Hello, Matilda. How are you today?" As curious as he was to find out what she'd wanted to tell him—what she thought could ruin everything—he knew this wasn't the time or place.

"I'm so excited that I can't stand it!" she said with a giggle. "I haven't told Johnny anything except that he's getting a fantastic surprise. I wanted you to be the one to tell him."

"I can hear you, you know," Johnny called from inside the room.

"Shall we?" Charon motioned toward the door and followed the giggling beauty into the room.

The boy sat on the bed beneath a blue blanket. He was propped up against pillows. Although his face was pale from prolonged illness, his dark brows, dark eyes, black hair, and steady jaw were handsome. His body was thin, as Charon had expected, but the boy possessed a confidence that made him seem less frail than he was.

"Johnny, this is Charon," Matilda said with a smile. "Charon, this is Johnny."

"So, what's this all about?" Johnny asked. "Have you found a cure?"

Charon frowned. "Unfortunately, no."

"I'm just pulling your chain," Johnny said with a laugh. "I know there's no cure."

Matilda moved to the other side of Johnny's bed, across from Charon. "Remember your bucket list?"

"What about it?" Johnny asked.

"Charon wants to help you with it," she said, unable to hold back. "His father left him a lot of money, and this is what he wants to do with it—or some of it, I guess. Isn't that awesome?"

Johnny frowned. "Does he know what's on my bucket list? He might change his mind."

"I'm up for anything," Charon said. "The sky's the limit."

"Why me?" Johnny asked. "You don't even know me."

"That's true," Charon said. "But I trust Matilda, and this is what she wants."

Tears filled Matilda's eyes. "Life works in mysterious ways. This is a blessing. Don't try to analyze it."

Johnny reached over to the side table drawer and pulled out a slip of paper. The creases made it look as though it had once been crumpled up and thrown away before someone had opened it and smoothed it out again. In pen, in sloppy print, appeared this list:

1. Zipline over the Amazon rain forest
2. Smoke pot in Amsterdam
3. Play the slots in Vegas
4. Parade down the streets of New Orleans
5. Steal a car
6. Pet a lion

"Well, I don't know about the last two," Charon said.

"What?" Johnny said with disappointment. "Dude, those are the most important."

"Why don't we start at the top and work our way down?" Charon suggested. "We'll see how it goes."

"You mean I probably won't make it to the end, anyway," Johnny said.

Charon was baffled by the boy's attitude, which seemed less than grateful.

"I wouldn't say that," Charon said, trying to hide his own disappointment. "We don't have to do anything at all, however, if you're not willing."

"Come on, Johnny," Matilda said. "I thought you'd be excited."

"*You* clearly are," Johnny said with a pout. "Why can't *you* come?"

"You know why," Matilda said.

"But I don't even know the guy," Johnny whispered.

Matilda leaned closer to the boy. "Let's be honest for a minute here. What have you got to lose?"

Charon was shocked that she would say such a thing to a dying boy. The boy seemed as surprised as Charon. He looked up at Matilda with his mouth hanging open.

"I'm not trying to be mean, Johnny," she said. "But this is a great opportunity for you to go out and experience the world. Does it matter who takes you?"

Johnny glanced at Charon. "You really want to blow your money on *me*?"

"It's just money," Charon said. "I don't care anything about it, to be honest."

"Said anyone without it *never*," Johnny muttered.

"Don't be rude," Matilda scolded.

"Look who's talking," the boy said.

Charon looked across the bed at Matilda. "Maybe this was a bad idea."

"Maybe it was," the boy said. "Why don't you just go? Both of you."

"Johnny," Matilda began gently.

Johnny closed his eyes and shouted, "Just go."

Matilda crossed to Charon's side and took his hand, whispering, "I'm sorry," as she led him from the room.

"Wait!" Johnny cried.

Charon and Matilda stepped back through the door. Charon wasn't sure what to make of the boy's face. It was twisted in despair, and he was sobbing.

"Do you really think the doctor would let me zipline?" Johnny asked.

Matilda rushed to his bedside and put her arms around him. "Of course, she would. I know she would."

Then, so quietly that a mortal standing in Charon's position would not have heard, the boy whispered to Matilda, "I'm not worth it—all the time and money he's offering to spend. I'm not worth it."

Matilda stroked the boy's black hair and said, "Yes, you most certainly are, Johnny Trevino. And much more than that."

Matilda kissed the boy's cheek and held him as he wept, while Charon stood near the door, at a loss. The boy's emotions confused and overwhelmed the ferryman. He wondered if he'd made a mistake in offering to help. How would he handle the moody boy without Matilda?

* * *

"I've never been on a plane before," Johnny said in the seat beside Charon before liftoff.

"Neither have I," Charon said.

Johnny wrinkled his nose. "Get out of here."

Charon glanced around the crowded plane. "Where should I go?"

"You've never flown before?" the boy asked with incredulous eyes.

"Yes. Many times. Just not on a plane."

"Huh? You mean, like a helicopter?"

"Chariot, mostly."

Johnny laughed. "Yeah, right."

The air was stuffy, and so were most of the people crammed together with Charon and the boy. People avoided eye contact and were short with one another when they spoke. The god was reminded why he didn't particularly care for people.

"God-travel would be so much easier," Charon muttered.

When the plane took off, Johnny grabbed Charon's wrist. The boy let go as quickly as he'd grabbed it and flushed with embarrassment when Charon met his eyes.

"I don't know what I'm worried about," Johnny said as they lifted into the air. "It's going to happen one way or another."

Charon wasn't sure what to say to that, so he said nothing. Instead, he dwelled on what Matilda had told him when they'd been alone the previous afternoon at lunch, sorting out the details of the trip. She'd finally told him what she'd feared might ruin everything. She'd confessed that she thought it was possible to bring someone back from the dead, and she was determined to do it one day.

Although it hadn't ruined everything, it had certainly shocked Charon to learn that the sweet and beautiful Matilda was dabbling with necromancy, the one thing Charon could never tolerate. He'd told her that only black magic could make such a thing possible.

She'd frowned and had said, "I guess that's a matter of perspective."

They'd been dining at the same coffee and sandwich shop as they'd eaten when she'd read the tarot.

"I'm telling you it's risky business," he'd said. "Why in the world would you ever want to do such a thing?"

"I want to bring my mother back," she'd said.

Later, after the plane had stabilized in the air, the boy interrupted Charon's thoughts by asking, "You got any kids?"

"No. I never married."

"You're still young. I can tell you like Matilda."

Charon smiled for the first time since they'd boarded. It was true—despite her interest in the dark art of necromancy. "Yes."

"Think you might want to marry her some day?"

"I'm sure I would, but it wouldn't be possible."

Johnny leaned back and lifted his chin. "Why not?"

"We're too different."

"You mean because you're white and she's black?"

"Not at all," Charon said. "Why does that matter?"

"Then why?"

"You wouldn't understand."

They were quiet again until the flight attendant took their drink orders.

Then Johnny asked, "So tell me where you're from and stuff, or are you worried about getting too close to someone like me?"

Charon bent his brows. "Like you?"

"You know. Someone terminal."

"That doesn't worry me." Then he added, "And it shouldn't worry you."

"You're right, man. It's not like I'm leaving anyone behind. No one will even notice."

"Matilda will miss you."

"I have a sister, but I don't know where she is."

"When was the last time you saw her?" Charon asked.

"We were together until I was seven and she was six, and then we got separated in the foster system. I wish I could see her, you know, to say goodbye. Matilda's tried to find her, but I guess it's impossible."

"What's her name?"

"Jessie. Jessica. I don't know her last name. We were both Trevino for a while, but we weren't born with that name. It was given to me by my last foster family."

"I see. Well, maybe I can help you look for her."

"Do you have any brothers or sisters?" Johnny asked.

"One of each."

"And do you see them often?"

"Almost never."

"How come?"

Charon was beginning to feel irritated by Johnny's questions. Would they never end? "I guess we're all too busy. We drifted apart. Went our separate ways."

"Yeah, that happens."

Their drinks came, along with a bag of pretzels for each of them. Johnny was quiet again while he ate and drank and gazed through the window at the white clouds below. It was going to be a long flight.

Then, nearly an hour later, as Charon was trying to work out how he might convince Matilda to accept her mother's death, Johnny suddenly said, "I'm sorry about your dad. Matilda told me."

Charon thought of Bill. He hadn't known the dog long, but he'd known him long enough to develop strong feelings for him. No one had ever been so affectionate toward Charon—not even his mother. "I miss him."

"He's lucky," Johnny said before he grew sullen again. "It must be nice to be missed."

Chapter 7

Hours later, Charon and Johnny camped in Peru by the Sacsara River. Their campfire was on a rocky embankment wedged between mountains beneath a blanket of stars. They sat on logs with their guides—a husband and wife named Roderigo and Victoria, who spoke of the food they would cook in the morning. Yards away, beneath a canopy of trees, Charon and Johnny would sleep in a treehouse until early morning, when they would zipline over the rain forest.

After the husband and wife said goodnight, Charon and Johnny were left alone. Charon wasn't sleepy and waited for Johnny to decide when they would retire to the treehouse. They sat quietly staring at the crackling fire.

"Do *you* have a bucket list?" Johnny asked him.

"I can't say that I do," Charon admitted.

Johnny gave him a sideways glance. "I guess you never think about death."

"I think about him often enough."

"Huh?"

Charon decided not to explain that Death was a person. Instead, he said, "There's no reason to be afraid."

"That's easy for you to say."

"I suppose it is."

"It sucks having to wait around for it to happen, you know? A quick death would be better." Then Johnny added, "Slow and steady doesn't always win the race."

"Sounds like you're anxious for Death—not reluctant for him—er, it."

"Only because I'm sick of worrying about it every minute of the day. I just want it to be over. Except..."

"Except what?"

Johnny folded his arms across his chest. "What if this is it, you know? What if when we die, it's the end for us?"

"I promise you, it's not the end," Charon said.

"You can't know that. None of us can."

"I can't tell you how, but I know," Charon insisted. "The souls cross into the Underworld where they're judged and sentenced to one of three places: The Elysian Fields, Tartarus, or Erebus."

"You read that in a book."

Charon didn't know what to say. There was no way he could convince the boy without divulging his identity.

But the boy gave him no chance to reply. "You really believe that?"

"I do," Charon said.

"Wish I could."

Charon sighed. "Why dwell on it? Either you do live on, or you don't. If you do, you'll see I'm right. If you don't, you won't know it, anyway."

Johnny stared blankly at the fire, as though he was processing what he'd been told.

"The hardest part of dying isn't what happens after," Charon said. "Unless you're condemned to suffer in Tartarus, which wouldn't be the case for you, I wouldn't think."

"I think you're wrong."

"I highly doubt that, Johnny. What could you have done that would land you in Tartarus?"

Johnny avoided the question by asking, "If the hardest part of dying isn't what happens after, then what is?"

"It's the anticipation," Charon said. "What you're dealing with right now. And my job is to help you to stop anticipating it by reminding you that you still have things to do while you're here. Let's just focus on what we're doing now and not what's coming later. Can you do that?"

"I guess I can try."

"Good." Charon smiled. "Now, tell me. Can you name any of the constellations?"

* * *

After a delicious breakfast, Charon and Johnny were fitted into hats, gloves, and harnesses before they followed Victoria and Rodrigo up the steep, twenty-minute climb through trees and over streams to the zipline. At the top of the hill, which was part of a much larger mountain, they climbed several metal steps to a platform that looked out over the valley below. They were well above the treetops of the forest and could even see the Sacsara River twisting through the rocky hills.

Worried that the climb had been too rigorous for Johnny, Charon asked the boy if he was okay.

"Never better," he replied.

The guides led them to two parallel ziplines that sloped down to a platform invisible from here, deep inside the trees.

As the guides hooked Charon and Johnny's harnesses to each of the lines and prepared them for their adventure, the boy seemed frightened and less exhilarated than Charon had thought he would be.

"We don't have to do this, if you don't want to," Charon said to the boy.

"We've come this far," Johnny said through chattering teeth. "You've gone to all this trouble."

"Never mind that," Charon said. "We've had a good time of it, anyway, haven't we? Even without this part."

"Yeah, I guess. But what would I tell Matilda?"

"Whatever you want."

"It's not as bad as you think, once you get going," Victoria said. "I'd hate for you to miss out."

"It's up to the boy," Rodrigo said.

"Has anyone ever fallen?" Johnny asked.

"Never," Victoria said.

"We use only the best equipment," Rodrigo added.

Johnny took a deep breath. "What have I got to lose? Let's do it. Now, before I change my mind."

Victoria pushed Johnny from the platform, and he soared, shrieking above the treetops. Charon quickly followed.

Although hanging from a wire was not a big treat to a god who could fly, Charon had to admit that the view from here was incredible. Charon's flights had been limited to the dark caverns of the Underworld and a few rare trips to Mount Olympus by chariot. He'd never seen such a variety of plant and animal life. The fact that it was all framed by a bright, blue sky, shiny mountains, sparkling river, and colorful foliage made it all the more exceptional.

"How are you doing, Johnny?" Charon called from where he soared a few feet behind the boy.

"It's awesome!" Johnny shouted. "Totally awesome!"

Charon was relieved that the boy was happy. The ferryman didn't know why, but the boy's happiness had become very important to him.

* * *

The streets of Amsterdam were slick with rain as Charon followed Johnny down the sidewalk among the other pedestrians. The sky had cleared after lunchtime, bringing a chilly wind that made forty degrees feel more like thirty. Johnny pulled his jacket around him but otherwise showed no sign of discomfort. He'd seemed happy and lighthearted ever since the zipline.

Johnny stopped and pointed to a corner coffeehouse. "Let's try that one. It looks interesting."

"Lead the way," Charon said.

They walked around two parked bicycles and a woman nursing a baby on an outdoor bench before they entered the little shop. It was filled with smoke, which somewhat obscured the view of the interesting art covering the walls. An abstract sculpture, as large as a man, took up the center of the space, around which square metal tables and chairs were clustered. A dozen other patrons sat at tables smoking, eating, and drinking coffee.

"This looks like the right place," Johnny said.

They approached the counter, where they were shown a menu.

The woman behind the counter asked, in Dutch, "What may I serve you today?"

Johnny looked back at the woman blankly, but Charon, able to communicate with all beings, replied in Dutch, "Two coffees and two pure joints, please."

Charon followed Johnny to a table near the window facing the street, so they could watch the passersby.

"I didn't know you could speak Dutch," Johnny said.

"I speak many languages." He'd decided not to divulge that he spoke *every* language.

"Have you ever smoked pot before?" Johnny asked before he took a drag.

"Never. You?"

"Yeah. It got me kicked out of my last foster home."

"Oh, that's too bad."

"I didn't like them anyway," Johnny said. "They couldn't accept me. They made me feel bad about who I am."

"In what way?" Charon asked.

"They made me watch a movie about how gays are sinners, and how those who overcome it go to heaven. It was bullshit, but they believed in it, and they expected me to believe in it, too."

"Sexuality has nothing to do with where a soul is taken in the afterlife," Charon said.

"I agree, but that family doesn't accept gays. I begged my caseworker to move me to another placement, but there wasn't anything available. I knew if I got caught with a joint, they'd kick me out, and they did."

"Good riddance," Charon said before taking another drag.

Then Charon heard the boy's unwitting prayer to him: *What a relief. You don't hate gays. That would have been awkward.*

"Why did it matter that we came to Amsterdam?" Charon asked as he blew smoke up toward the ceiling and watched it curl above him.

Johnny shrugged. "It sounded fun, I guess. Different, you know?"

Charon believed he did know. "I doubt this joint will affect me much. I feel very little from alcohol, and I imagine I'll feel even less from this. But when in Rome..."

"That's too bad," Johnny said. "I can already feel it. It's very nice."

"I'm glad to see you happy," Charon said.

Johnny laughed. "I wouldn't go that far. But, yeah. Thanks."

After a while, Charon *did* begin to feel the effects of the weed. He sat back in his chair and stretched out his legs, because he felt like he was floating.

"I'm still sitting down, aren't I?" he asked Johnny.

The boy's lids were half closed. "Yeah, man. I think so." He laughed. "Why? Are you high?"

"I feel high, yes," Charon said. "And that's saying something, since, well, since I can fly."

Johnny busted out with laughter, throwing his head back. "You really are high, man. You're flying, alright."

"Oh, no, no, no, I mustn't," Charon said with a frown. "I can't divulge who I am. Am I still flying? Or have I landed yet?"

Still laughing, Johnny said, "Who are you then? The man in the moon?"

"There's no *man* in the moon. Only a woman, a goddess named Selene. The man, my boy, is in the sun. Helios."

The boy snorted more laughter and, with a teasing look, pointed at Charon. "If you're not the man in the moon, then who are you?"

Charon leaned across the table, not sure whether he was touching ground. "You must promise not to tell a soul, not even Matilda."

Johnny now leaned over the table, too. "I promise."

"I'm a god from the Underworld," Charon said.

Johnny threw his head back again and let out the most delightful sound. Charon did the same.

Chapter 8

Two days later, Charon and Johnny met Matilda in Las Vegas, where she had arranged for the three of them to stay for the weekend at a spectacular hotel called the Excalibur. Charon and Johnny's flight arrived first, and, as they waited at the gate for Matilda's flight to land, they were both in a good mood.

"Don't forget what you said," Charon told Johnny. "What happened in Amsterdam stays in Amsterdam."

Johnny winked. "No worries, Charon. I got your back."

Charon could tell that Johnny hadn't believed him when he'd said he was a god, but he'd rather the boy kept quiet about it, anyway.

When Matilda entered from the gate, Charon was reminded of how beautiful she was. It wasn't that he'd forgotten, exactly; but, she seemed to have a glow about her that magnified it. As usual, she wore her curly black hair down and pinned behind her ears. The hairstyle showed off her lovely cheek bones and those mesmerizing black eyes.

"I'm so excited!" she said as she threw her arms, first around Johnny's neck and then around Charon's.

Charon was caught off guard by the embrace. Flustered and dumbstruck, he was relieved when Johnny took over the conversation.

"I can't wait to tell you what we've been up to," Johnny said.

"Let's get out of here, so you can tell me all about it," Matilda said.

"What about your luggage?" Charon asked, finally finding his tongue.

"I have everything I need in this." She indicated the colorful bag strapped over her shoulder. "Come on!"

* * *

Once they were settled in their rooms—Charon and Johnny in one and Matilda in another next door—Matilda came over and closed the door behind her.

She handed a card to Johnny, who was seated on one of two beds. "This fake ID won't work without a glamour spell."

"A what?" the boy asked.

Charon hadn't realized how advanced Matilda's skills were. A glamour spell would allow her to make mortals see an illusion. He crossed the room and pulled the curtains closed.

"I'm going to make you look older," she explained. "If they know you're a minor, you won't be allowed on the floors where the machines are."

Johnny's eyes widened. "I didn't know you could do that."

"I'm not sure if I can," she said. "But it's worth a try, isn't it?"

Johnny gave a nervous laugh. "As long as you don't turn me into a frog."

She put her shoulder bag on the bed and pulled out a candle, setting it on the desk. Beside it she placed a rock the size of a golf ball and a dried sprig of purple flowers.

"What's that?" Charon asked, pointing to the flowers.

"Vervain." She took a salt shaker and sprinkled salt on the desk beside the other items before using a lighter to set a flame to the candlewick. "There. Now I just need a cup of water." She took one of the hotel

72

glasses and handed it to Charon. "Do you mind? Just fill it halfway at the bathroom sink."

He did as he was told. When he returned from the bathroom, Johnny was seated at the desk, with his hands on the rock, sprig of Vervain, and salt. Matilda took the glass of water and put it in the center of her arrangement beside the candle.

"If this doesn't work, will I not be able to play?" Johnny asked.

"We'll still try to get you on a machine," Matilda reassured him "But if this works, it'll be easier to get away with it."

"Then let's hope it works," Johnny said.

"I need you to close your eyes and concentrate," she said to Johnny.

Charon stood behind Matilda and watched, only half believing she could manage it, as she said:

Fire, herb, water, salt, rock, hear me as my song is sung. Youth is not his heart's desire. To adulthood he does aspire. Fire, herb, water, salt, rock. Tick, tock, tick, tock.

Matilda then put the rock, Vervain, and salt into the cup of water before she turned the candle upside down and extinguished the flame. A silvery smoke rose up from the glass and surrounded Johnny.

With wide eyes, Matilda whispered, "It's working!"

To Charon, Johnny was unchanged; but, he knew such spells didn't work on gods, so he played along. "How incredible."

Johnny jumped up from the chair to gaze at himself in the bathroom mirror. Charon followed and was surprised by the look of disbelief on the boy's reflection.

"This is insane," the boy muttered, apparently in shock.

"You look older than me!" Matilda said with a laugh.

"I didn't think such a thing possible," Johnny mumbled.

"I'm not sure how long it'll last," Matilda said, "so, we better get a move on."

They took the elevator to the main level, where they bought Johnny a two-hundred-dollar voucher to use in the slot machines. Charon was pleased that whenever he opened the wallet given to him by Thanatos, more dollars appeared inside. It seemed he would never run out of cash.

As the boy ran off to have his fun, Matilda and Charon sat together at a table near the bar. Charon still wasn't used to the attention of the ladies, but he got quite a lot of their stares and smiles. He didn't know how to handle it, so he just ignored them.

Once they each had a drink in hand, Charon asked Matilda, "What other spells can you do?"

She gave him a coy grin. "A witch never gives away her secrets."

Charon took a swig of his whiskey.

"I can do quite a few," she said. "Mostly spells of convenience—like a location spell for something lost, or a memory spell when I need to memorize information for school."

"Can you do a location spell to find the boy's sister?" Charon asked.

"He's told you about her?"

Charon nodded.

"I wish I could. I've tried, many times, but I need to burn something that once belonged to her, and Johnny doesn't have anything of hers. He doesn't even have anything of his own. The poor things have nothing."

"They once had each other," Charon said. "It's too bad they were separated."

Matilda's mouth dropped open and a dazed look came over her.

"What is it?"

"You're a genius!" she said before she kissed his cheek.

Heat rushed to his face and to his abdomen. He'd never been kissed before—not even by his mother or sister. It was a peculiar feeling, in a wonderful kind of way. He hoped it would happen again.

"I can use *him* for the location spell!" she said. "Because he belongs to her, just like you said."

"I don't understand. How can you use him? You can't burn him."

"Sure, I can," she said with a mischievous smile.

* * *

A few hours later, Johnny found them at their table.

"I was four hundred dollars up," he said. "But then I blew it. Every penny."

"No worries," Charon said.

"The point is, did you have fun?" Matilda asked.

Johnny grinned. "Totally. But now what? We have all day tomorrow, too, and I've blown my gambling budget in three hours."

"There's plenty more to do," Matilda said. "But it's a good thing you've finished gambling. My spell has worn off, hasn't it Charon?"

Since Charon couldn't tell the difference, he played along. "You're back to yourself, young man."

Matilda stood up from the table. "Let's go have some fun!"

She led them to the elevator and down to the basement, to what was called the Fun Dungeon. There they found carnival games, an arcade, and 4-D amusement experiences.

The 4-D amusement experiences bewildered Charon. They were like the cinema combined with a fast-pace train ride. At one point, when the illusion of a boulder crashing into him made him panic, he accidentally god-traveled out of his seat. He returned in less than a second and prayed to Hades that no one noticed.

That evening, they ate a Medieval-style dinner in the hotel theater-in-the-round arena, where they watched an interactive, live performance called *The Tournament of Kings*. Knights in colorful armor rode horseback and carried lances. The audience was called on to cheer for the knight closest to them. Charon enjoyed the experience tremendously and could tell his companions felt the same, until suddenly Johnny's face became pale as he clutched his stomach.

"Johnny?" Matilda put an arm around him.

"I think I'm going to be sick," he muttered.

"Let's go back to the room," Charon suggested.

He helped Johnny from the theater. As they took the elevator up to their rooms, Johnny vomited on the elevator floor.

"I'm sorry," he said.

"Don't apologize," Matilda said. "They'll send someone to clean it up right away."

"You have no reason to be sorry," Charon said as the elevator doors opened.

A group of people waiting to board saw the mess and frowned.

"You'll want to take another elevator," Charon said to them as he helped Johnny into the hall.

Johnny threw up once more in the toilet before laying down on his bed.

Matilda pressed a wet cloth to his forehead. "Feel any better yet?"

He nodded. "Sorry to ruin the evening."

Charon sat on edge of the other bed. "You didn't ruin it. If it weren't for you, I never would have come to this place and known about the fun to be had here. So, stop apologizing."

Johnny gave a wry laugh. "That's nice of you to say, but I'm calling bullshit."

Charon lifted his brows and glanced at Matilda. He had no idea what the boy meant. Matilda's laughter didn't help, either.

"Listen," Matilda said to Johnny. "Charon gave me an idea. You know how I've been trying to think of a way to use a location spell to find your sister?"

Johnny nodded.

"Since you're her brother, you belong to her, in a way," Matilda explained. "I'd like to try burning a lock of your hair."

Johnny opened his eyes wide. "You think that would work?"

"There's only one way to find out," Matilda said with a wink. "I'll be right back."

Charon and Johnny exchanged glances as Matilda left the room.

"She likes you, you know," Johnny said.

"I like her, too," Charon said.

"No, I mean, *likes* likes."

"I don't know what that means."

"Dude," Johnny rolled his eyes. "Do you live under a rock, or what?"

"In a matter of speaking," Charon mumbled.

"It means she's falling for you, man," Johnny said. "I think she's falling in love with you."

Charon couldn't think of what to say to that, but it didn't matter, because in the next moment, Matilda returned with her bag. She placed four blue candles in a circle on the desk. Then she filled the ice bucket with water in the bathroom and set it in the center of the circle. She lit each candle and a dried sprig of another flower.

"This is Jasmine," she said, before Charon could ask. She let the dry sprig burn for a moment before she blew out the flame and set it, smoking, in an empty glass. Then she turned to Johnny. "I just need a single strand of your hair."

Johnny tugged a few black hairs from his head and handed them over.

Matilda pulled something made of paper from her bag. "This is a world map. I've got a few of them in my bag of tricks. You'll see why in a minute."

Next, Matilda held the strands of hair over the flame on one of the candles.

"Oh, no!" She turned to Charon. "The hair won't hold a flame."

"I could have told you that," Johnny said.

"It just melts away. Singes, really." Matilda frowned. "I need something that will hold a flame, if only for an instant."

"What about a toenail?" Charon suggested.

"I guess we could try it." Matilda searched through her bag and took out a pair of scissors. Then she pulled off one of Johnny's shoes and socks.

"Be careful," Johnny said. "If I get an infection..."

"I'll be careful," Matilda said with a reassuring smile. "Now let's have a look at your big toe."

78

Johnny sighed and closed his eyes. "This isn't going to work."

In another moment, Matilda held a clipping of Johnny's toenail with a pair of tweezers. "Let the experiment commence."

Charon stood and looked over her shoulder as she held the toenail to one of the flames. At first, the end just curled and charred, and Charon thought it was another failure; but, then, a flame burst in the center of the clipping. Matilda grabbed the world map and held it to the flame, but the flame went out.

"Is that supposed to happen?" Charon asked.

Matilda shook her head. "The map needs to catch fire and burn using a flame from an object once belonging to the person we're looking for."

"Told ya," Johnny said.

"Try again," Charon said, wanting badly to help the mortals. He'd never wanted anything more. "He has ten toenails and ten fingernails. Let's not give up until we've exhausted them all."

"Even if I get the flame to light the map," Matilda said, "there's no guarantee that the spell will work. I'm basing this on the idea that Johnny belongs to his sister."

"What have we got to lose?" Charon pointed out.

"Just don't cut me," Johnny said. "One infection is all it would take to do me in."

"I won't cut you," Matilda said. "But we don't have to do this if you don't feel comfortable."

Johnny sucked on his lips and seemed to be deliberating.

"Your nails look like they could use a trim, anyway," Charon said.

This made Johnny smile. "Alright, then. Go ahead."

Matilda beamed at Charon, the excitement and hope clear on her face. That feeling of being in cahoots with someone, of working together toward a common goal, felt exciting and wonderful—especially since that someone was the kind and beautiful Matilda.

The next two toenail clippings were also failures, but then Matilda decided to try holding several clippings in the tweezers at once, and this produced a flame long enough to make the map catch fire.

"Thank Hecate!" Matilda shouted.

Charon's jaw dropped open. "What did you say?"

"Thank Hecate," she repeated. "She's the goddess of witches. I pray to her for help with my spells."

Charon knew very well who Hecate was. She was the companion to Persephone and spent half of every year in the Underworld. He was merely surprised that Matilda knew of her, and even more surprised that she believed in her and prayed to her. Most mortals these days considered the gods to be nothing but the stuff of myths.

Once the map was engulfed in flames, Matilda dropped it into the bucket full of water. Charon watched over her shoulder as the flame was replaced by smoke.

Matilda used her finger to stir the water as she said, "Please show me the location of Johnny Trevino's sister, Jessica."

A small piece of the map, about a square-inch in size and with singed edges, floated to the top of the water. Matilda picked it out of the ice bucket and held it beneath the desk lamp.

"Did it work?" Johnny asked eagerly from the bed. "What does it say?"

"It's the state of California," Matilda said.

"Great," Johnny moaned. "How does that help?"

"This is a good sign," Matilda reassured him. "If the spell had given us Nevada, we would have known it was pointing to you."

"But how can we find Jessie just by knowing she's in California?" Johnny complained. "I'm pretty sure we already knew that."

"We do the spell again," Matilda said. "Using a California map. That will tell us what city."

"Then what?" Charon asked.

"We repeat the spell with a city map," she explained. "To find the street or neighborhood."

"And then go knocking door to door?" Johnny asked sarcastically.

Matilda laughed. "Ye of little faith! From there, we use a different spell and follow the smoke. You'll see." She sat on the bed next to Johnny. "Trust me. We'll find your sister."

"Unless I run out of finger and toenails first," Johnny said.

"Why don't we let the boy rest for the night," Charon suggested. "I'll go look for a California map, and we'll continue this in the morning."

"I'll go with you," Matilda said.

Charon glanced back at Johnny and was taken aback when the boy gave him a knowing look that was followed by a silent prayer: *See? I told you she liked you.*

It was all the ferryman could do not to blush with embarrassment as he followed Matilda to the door.

"Call me on my cell if you need anything," Matilda told Johnny. "We won't be far."

Johnny saluted her. "Aye, aye, captain."

When they were alone in the hallway and were headed toward the elevators, Charon asked her, "Do you really believe you can find his sister?"

"I don't know," she said. "I hope so. He felt responsible for her when they were young. He protected her, and he's never recovered from being torn apart from her. It would be the best gift we could give him to reunite them before he goes."

"I hope it works. I'd hate for him to be disappointed."

"Life is full of disappointments," she said.

"True enough."

"But we have to aim high, don't you think?" she quickly added. "Even at the risk of great disappointments?"

Once they'd reached the elevators, she turned to study his face. He heard her unwitting prayer to him: *God, you're beautiful.*

He gaped for a moment before he collected himself. Then he said, "Yes. We must aim high."

Charon and Matilda walked two blocks down the Las Vegas strip to a Walgreen's, and when they found no California map there, they crossed the street toward CVS. Charon decided to take this opportunity to ask her why she wanted to bring her mother back from the dead.

"She wasn't supposed to die," Matilda said as he held the door to CVS open for her to step inside.

He followed her into the store. "Few people believe they're supposed to die."

"But she really wasn't. I was."

He followed her down an aisle and watched her peruse the few maps.

"No California maps here, either," she said.

In a low voice, so as not to be overheard by other shoppers, he asked, "Does Johnny need to be present for you to perform the location spell?"

"I guess not," she said.

"Maybe you can keep working on it when you get back. Take the nail clippings with you."

"I suppose that's what I'll have to do. Should we head back?"

"I think so. I don't like leaving the boy alone for too long."

As they walked down the strip in the cool night, dodging others, some of which were drunk, Charon asked Matilda what she'd meant when she'd said she was supposed to die.

"I had leukemia, like Johnny. My mom did a spell, without telling me, of course. I never would have let her do it."

"She switched fates with you," Charon said.

Matilda nodded. "It's refreshing to talk to someone who understands these things."

Charon gave her a reassuring smile.

"Anyway," she continued. "It wasn't her time to go. It was mine."

Charon took her arm and stopped in the middle of the sidewalk, turning to face her. "Listen to me, Matilda. You won't be able to bring her back unless you switch with her again. The only way to resurrect your mother without black magic is for you to die in her place."

She wrinkled her brow and gazed up at him— her mouth so close that he could almost touch her lips with his. "What makes you such an expert on death and resurrection?"

He stared back at her, unable to find the words.

If only she knew.

"Well?" she asked. "Have you studied witchcraft since you were a baby?"

"No…"

"That's what I thought. Now let's go."

They walked in silence for another block, but, when they reached the hotel, she grabbed his hand and stopped him from entering the building.

"I'm sorry," she said, still holding his hand. "I didn't mean to get short with you. It's a touchy subject for me. I hope you understand."

He squeezed her hand. "I do."

He was about to turn and open the door for her when she reached up and held his cheek. Everything in his body froze, except his heart, which pounded fast and hard. At that moment, he wanted nothing more than to kiss her. His wish came true when she pressed her mouth to his.

Of their own accord, his arms wrapped around her thin waist. He could no longer think as he pulled her into him and ravished her lips with his.

"Get a room!" an old woman said as she walked past them toward the hotel.

Perplexed, Charon said to her, "We have rooms, thank you."

"Then use one!" the woman shouted as she entered the building.

Matilda laughed out loud—a hard laugh, from deep in her belly. Seeing her in hysterics made him laugh, too. Together, they followed the old woman into the hotel lobby and continued to giggle all the way up to their rooms.

Chapter 9

On the plane to New Orleans, Charon lay back in his seat reliving the weekend in Vegas with the beautiful Matilda, over and over in his mind. Johnny sat beside him, but Matilda had flown to Los Angeles, back to work and school.

It had only been a few hours since he'd said goodbye to her in the airport, and he already couldn't wait to see her again.

Charon was brought from his thoughts by the sound of sobs. It was Johnny. His eyes were red, his face twisted in despair. When he rubbed his eyes, his hands trembled.

"Johnny?" Charon asked.

"I don't deserve this. Any of it."

"Life isn't fair," Charon said. "Only Death is." That was what Hades had always said. Charon had learned it from his master.

"What the hell are you talking about?" Johnny said, wiping his tears with his fists.

"The things that happen to you while you're alive are rarely ever fair and just," Charon said. "Especially the way you die. But what happens in Death, in the Underworld—whether you go to the Elysian Fields, to Tartarus, or to Erebus—that's fair. Hades, the lord of the Underworld, has made sure of it. His Kingdom is the most just one of all."

"Oh, you're regurgitating stuff you've read in books to me again, are you?"

"I'm just saying that you're right. You don't deserve to have cancer."

"No, I don't mean the stupid cancer," Johnny said. "That I *do* deserve. I mean you and Matilda. What you're doing for me." He struggled to speak against the sobs. "All the money you're spending on me. It could go to something better."

Charon lifted his brows. "Why would you say such a thing? You've been struck with this terrible illness that's cutting your life short. Why shouldn't you enjoy as much of what you have left as you can? And why shouldn't I help you?"

"Because I'm a rotten person, that's why." Johnny closed his eyes and covered his face as his whole body shuddered.

"I disagree," Charon said.

"Because you don't know me," Johnny said. "You don't know what I've done."

"Then tell me, so I can make a more informed opinion."

Johnny rubbed his eyes and took a deep breath. "I did something bad to one of my foster families."

"When did your parents die?"

"Jessie and I were taken away from our mother when I was four and Jessie was three. Our mother was a drug addict. We never knew what happened to our father."

Charon frowned. He'd experienced these kinds of stories before from the souls that boarded his skiff. Drugs had destroyed lives as often as disease and poverty. "Have you seen your mother since?"

"No, but I was told she killed herself not long after we were taken away."

"How sad," Charon muttered.

"After a year with our first foster mom, who I always think of when I think of 'Mom' because she was the sweetest, kindest…" Johnny broke off.

Charon patted the boy's arm. "Take your time, Johnny."

"She couldn't keep us," he said. "She never meant to keep us. She was just trying to help until we could find our forever home. But she already had five kids of her own, and she couldn't keep us."

Charon felt like his heart might crumble into bits. How could one mortal be expected to endure such pain and agony in such a short life?

"So, after a year with Mom, Jessie and I were moved to another foster home—an older couple whose own kids were in college. They were nice enough, but they couldn't handle us, I guess. After a few months, our caseworker showed up with two trash bags and told us to pack all our things in them. We weren't told why. And we didn't even have enough stuff to fill two trash bags."

"It sounds to me like you more than deserve what Matilda and I are doing for you."

Johnny shuddered. "Wait until you've heard the whole story."

"I'm listening. Go on."

"For the next few years, Jessie and I lived with the Trevino family," Johnny said. "At first, I was so happy to be a part of a real family, with three other brothers and another sister. Our foster mom and dad were nice. But, after a while, my foster brothers started to become more and more cruel to me. They called me gay, faggot, and queer. I hadn't come out yet—I wasn't even sure what I was. I was only six, but I was already different, I guess.

"When I was seven, one of my foster brothers wrote 'faggot' on my backpack in permanent marker. I begged my foster parents to give me a different backpack to take to school, but they said I should scratch it out and not take it seriously, that their son had only been joking and that I shouldn't let it get to me. But even after I scratched it out, I still felt like I was wearing a label that meant everyone hated me, that I was a nothing, a nobody, and totally worthless."

Charon squeezed Johnny's hand. "But you aren't worthless. You are someone. You're a somebody."

"That night, I, I..." Johnny took another deep breath. "I set my foster family's house on fire, and I got Jessie to run away with me."

"Was anyone killed in the fire?" Charon asked.

"No, but the house was totally destroyed. When they found me, I couldn't look any of them in the eye. I was put in juvie..."

"Juvie?"

"You know, a group home for juvenile delinquents."

"Oh, I see."

"And Jessie was moved to a different foster family. I never saw her or heard from her again after that."

"You were only seven years old," Charon said. "One mistake as a troubled youth does not define your worth as a human being."

"But everyone is always saying that our actions define us," Johnny said through trembling lips.

"The key being actions, plural," Charon said. "One action alone defines no one. What other actions have you done to neutralize that terrible one?"

Johnny opened his eyes wide and then closed them again. "Nothing. I haven't done anything except get sick and, soon, die."

"You aren't dead yet," Charon said.

"But what can I do?" Johnny asked.

"Let's think about it," Charon said. "Maybe an idea will come to us. Meanwhile, please stop carrying around this feeling that you're worthless. You haven't failed anyone; they've failed you. You don't deserve the cancer. No one deserves cancer. And you do deserve to have some fun. So, let's go have fun in New Orleans, and we'll think of something good you can do to balance out the bad. Okay, Johnny?"

Johnny wiped his eyes and smiled up at him. "Okay."

* * *

From their hotel balcony on the edge of the French Quarter, Charon and Johnny could see and hear a festival taking place across the busy main street. The hotel concierge had said it was the Treme Creole Gumbo Festival at Louis Armstrong Park. In the cab ride over from the airport, they'd seen a long, winding parade of jazz band players, people in strange and exotic costumes, dancing women in fancy dresses carrying parasols, and regular pedestrians marching together from the French Quarter to the park.

"Here's our chance," Charon said. "Shall we join them?"

"I'm worn out from the flight," Johnny said. "Can we rest for a bit first?"

"Of course, we can."

Johnny returned inside and made himself comfortable on one of the beds. Charon stayed on the balcony to watch the parade, but he left the balcony door open, so he could keep an eye on Johnny. Since they'd landed, the boy had seemed paler than normal and less energetic. Charon was worried.

It wasn't long before Johnny had fallen asleep. Charon crept quietly through the room, so as not to wake the boy, and into the bathroom to gaze at himself in the mirror.

He'd wondered how young he would become. Would he one day appear younger than even Johnny? The process seemed to come to a halt for the past several days, and now he supposed that he was as young-looking as he'd ever be, like a mortal in his mid-twenties.

He wondered what Hades and Persephone and the other Underworld gods would say when they saw him again. He missed his home—however much fun he was having here with his new friends. He missed his skiff and pole, the Acheron and the Styx, and, especially, the Phlegethon, the river of fire.

But he didn't miss the loneliness he'd only recently come to realize he'd been enduring for centuries. How would he ever go back to that?

And would he ever see the beautiful Matilda again? Or would he have to wait for the end of her life to see her, when her soul would board his skiff?

* * *

A few hours later, Johnny woke up and said he was feeling better. He said he was hungry, which Matilda had once indicated was a good sign. After freshening up, the two of them left the hotel and went to the streets to join the day-long parade to the festival.

The musicians played lively jazz music with their trumpets and trombones beneath a clear blue sky. Spicy aromas woke up Charon's taste buds and made him hungry, too. He and Johnny marched along North Rampart Street with the others to the crosswalk, where they headed toward the park. They crossed a bridge over a pond containing a beautiful fountain that sprayed water into the air.

Charon kept looking over at Johnny beside him to check how he was doing. His worries seemed to be for nothing, for the boy was smiling and dancing alongside others in the parade.

Dusk came, and, along with it, a chill, but the dimming day brought the festival lights to life. Booths lined the walkways, and their signs professed to have the best tasting gumbo around. Charon bought a bowl for each of them at one of the stands. The spicy goodness warmed Charon, and he finished the bowl in minutes.

Johnny said it was too much spice for him, so Charon bought him roasted corn.

They watched one of the bands perform on the stage at the center of the festival, but Charon could tell that Johnny was exhausted. He still looked paler and weaker than he'd been in recent days. For the first time since beginning the journey with him, Charon feared that they might not make it through the bucket list.

As much as Charon abhorred stealing, he understood something of the thrill that Johnny was hoping to gain from the experience of stealing a car. The boy wanted to borrow a car for a joy ride. Charon had the feeling the boy had gotten the idea from a movie, because he was sure it was portrayed to be much more thrilling on the screen than it was in real life. But Charon had said he would help the boy through the list, and he intended to keep his word.

There were plenty of cars parked along the streets of New Orleans. There were also crowds of people. Charon wasn't sure how they would succeed with the next item on Johnny's bucket list.

* * *

Back in their hotel room, Johnny made himself comfortable on the bed, to rest, while Charon sat in an upholstered chair opposite him.

Charon crossed one leg over the other. "If you're still determined to steal a car, we should do it here, in this crowded city, but only for a short time before we return it. Agreed?"

The boy took a sip of water from a glass on the stand beside his bed. "Okay, but there's something I want to tell you, first."

Charon lifted his brows. "I'm listening."

"First, promise me you won't be angry."

Charon wondered what the boy could possibly say that might anger him. He could think of nothing. "I won't be angry."

"Promise."

"I promise."

"You remember how I told you I was gay?"

"Of course, I remember."

"The thing is, I've never been kissed, except by my first foster mom, and that doesn't count. I've never been kissed romantically."

Until recently, neither had Charon. Matilda had been his first. "I know how you feel."

"I don't want to die before I see what that's like, you know?"

Charon leaned forward in his chair, resting his elbows on his knees. "I do know. I understand completely."

"So, I was wondering..." the boy hesitated, averting his eyes. "I know you and Matilda are a thing. I realize you're not gay. But I was hoping you might, I don't know, never mind. It's asking too much."

Charon finally understood what the boy was asking of him. "Of all the things on your bucket list, that seems the easiest one to accomplish."

Johnny's face brightened. "You mean you'll do it?"

"I'd be honored to, Johnny. I might not be the best kisser, since I don't have much experience." The best god for this task would have been Apollo, but Charon feared he'd summon the god too many times since he'd left.

"Dude, I'm sure it's fine. You're the most beautiful person I've ever met. Your looks will make up for what you might lack in that department."

"Well, that's comforting."

They both laughed.

Charon sat on the edge of the bed beside Johnny and held his face in his hands. He could sense the boy's fear, as well as his excitement, and, hoping to make it remarkable for the boy's sake, he decided not to rush it. He gazed into the boy's eyes and smiled warmly.

You are so incredibly beautiful, came Johnny's unwitting prayer. *And kind.*

"You're beautiful, too, Johnny. I'm glad I've had a chance to know you."

The boy stared up at him and said nothing. His eyes moved to Charon's lips.

Charon leaned down and pressed his mouth gently to Johnny's. He swept his lips back and forth across Johnny's before ending with a final kiss on the boy's cheek.

As Charon sat up and pulled away, Johnny closed his eyes and said, "Thank you. That was amazing. I can now die a happy man."

"But not today," Charon said.

"If you insist. But maybe I should sleep."

"Good night, then."

The boy opened his eyes and looked up again at Charon. "Thanks, man. I mean it. You've made my life."

"I've made it what?"

"You've *made* it. Period. Almost everything good about it happened after I met you."

"That's nice of you to say." To himself, he thought: *How sad.*

Johnny closed his eyes. "See you in the morning."

* * *

After a hot breakfast in the hotel restaurant, Charon and Johnny took a walk around the French Quarter, where they overheard guides giving tours in the streets. At least three different groups crossed their path. In all three cases, the guides spoke of ghosts and vampires.

Charon became interested in one story about the Ursuline Convent that went something like this: Because New Orleans was considered undesirable by the early French colonists, it was settled by criminals. Then, in the mid-seventeen-hundreds, the city, wishing to inject moral genes into the blood pool, brought nuns from France to be married off to its citizens. The young women arrived on ships, pale-faced from the long voyage, and with the blood-stained lips of tuberculosis. They carried wooden trunks resembling small caskets as they processed solemnly to their rooms in the convent. Rumors of the arrival of vampires became widespread among the townspeople.

Although Charon was certain that the convent contained no vampires, he did sense the presence of souls that had not been bound by Thanatos to the Underworld. These souls, or ghosts, were trapped here, unable to reach their final resting place. This saddened Charon, as he took his responsibility of ferrying the souls very seriously, because he knew it was important.

"Check it out." Johnny pointed to a red convertible parked on the corner in front of the convent.

"A nice chariot, indeed," Charon said.

"But look harder, at the steering column."

Charon had no idea what he was looking at. He knew little about cars and even less about driving them. "So?"

"Dude, the keys! The keys are in the ignition. This is our chance."

Charon glanced around at the crowds of pedestrians. "There are too many people."

"Dude," he whispered. "That's what we want. People will assume it's ours, and no one will be paying attention. Come on!"

The boy hopped into the passenger seat.

Charon stood on the sidewalk beside him. "You don't expect *me* to drive, do you?"

"Are you serious?" Johnny said through gritted teeth. "I don't have a license. I never learned."

"Neither did I."

"But you're, what, twenty-five? Thirty?" the boy asked, incredulous.

"I prefer public transportation," Charon lied.

"Just get in and try," Johnny pleaded.

"Believe me," Charon said. "We'll be much better off with you behind the wheel. Now scoot over, before someone comes."

Johnny moved behind the wheel, and Charon took his place in the passenger's seat.

"Buckle up," the boy said as he turned the key in the ignition and then strapped himself in.

Charon had no idea how to work the safety harness, so he left it dangling against the door as Johnny pulled from the curb. The street was narrow, and the pedestrians didn't always keep to the sidewalk, spilling into the narrow streets.

"Slow down," Charon warned. "And try not to hit anyone."

"This is so rad!" Johnny shouted. "I can't believe I'm driving!"

"Better not say that too loudly," Charon said. "Try not to draw attention to yourself."

They were coming up to a car that had stopped in front of them.

Again, Charon said, "Slow down. Stop!"

Johnny stepped on the brake, nearly throwing Charon from the vehicle.

"Put your seatbelt on, man! I told you, I don't know what I'm doing!"

Charon fiddled with the buckle until he figured it out. By then, the car in front of them had moved on, so Johnny stepped on the pedal. Charon couldn't remember ever being this frightened. He felt he'd put quite a few lives at risk by allowing Johnny to drive: other drivers, pedestrians, and Johnny himself. He needed to bring this adventure to a quick conclusion.

"Turn left up there," Charon said. "Circle around, and let's get the car back to where we found it."

"But we're just getting started!"

"Before you kill someone."

Johnny steered the car to the left, just as a woman pushing a stroller entered the street. To avoid them, Charon lifted the convertible into the air, shielding it from mortal eyes. Anyone watching would have seen a red convertible disappear into thin air.

"What the hell?" Johnny's eyes widened as he gripped the steering well. "Am I dead, or what?"

"You're not dead."

"What the hell is happening?" the boy asked as they floated over the street below.

"You nearly killed that woman and child," Charon said. "I couldn't be responsible for that."

"But, Dude! We're *flying*!" The boy's voice shot up several octaves on the word *flying*.

"Just promise you won't tell Matilda," Charon said.

Johnny searched Charon's face. "Tell Matilda what?"

Chapter 10

Two days later, they met Matilda at the San Diego Zoo. Johnny was still processing Charon's story about being a god from the Underworld, and, every so often, he'd ask Charon another question that had come to mind. The ferryman had answered each question truthfully, seeing no point in deceiving the boy any longer.

Johnny's questions had included: *How long have you been in existence? Can you read minds? What are the other gods like? How many are there? Is there life on other planets? Why haven't you ever married or had children? Why are you here? How long will you stay?*

He'd also asked harder questions: *Why do the gods allow illness, poverty, and starvation? Why don't they intervene when countries go to war?*

And then the hardest question of all: *Can you cure me and let me live? Please? I'll do anything.*

Charon had tried his best to explain why he had no power to change Johnny's fate, but the boy seemed unable to accept Charon's answer. There was a new tension between them. The boy resented a god who couldn't help him.

The boy had said, "What's the point of being a god if you have no power?"

Charon had replied, "I serve a purpose."

The boy had grown silent and sullen. After a while, Charon had come to believe that the boy would feel less sullen if he, too, had a purpose. Charon took it upon himself to help the boy discover his.

They'd been fortunate in their efforts to return the red convertible to its original parking place without incident; but, Johnny's new revelation about Charon had overshadowed the thrill of the experience and had left them both feeling on edge.

So, it was a great relief—to both of them, Charon imagined—when they were finally reunited with Matilda. She met them outside of the zoo entrance with their tickets in hand. She'd arranged for a special encounter for Johnny in the Elephant Odyssey Exhibit with the lions.

When they'd reached the exhibit, a zookeeper was feeding a large lioness through a chain-linked fence. Spectators had gathered behind a railing separating the zookeeper from the crowd. A second zookeeper stood beside the first holding a tub of meat. Matilda led Johnny and Charon through the spectators to the railing.

"Molly? It's Matilda," Matilda said.

"Oh, good!" the one who'd been feeding the lioness cried. She turned from the fence to face them. Her gloved hands were covered in blood. "I'm so glad you made it. Is this Johnny?"

"That's me," Johnny said.

Molly unlatched a gate through the railing. "Come on in, Johnny. Your parents, too."

"Oh, we aren't..." Matilda began with a red face as she glanced nervously at Charon. But she gave off explaining.

After Johnny, Matilda, and Charon had stepped through, Molly closed and latched the gate behind them.

"This is Etosha," she said, pointing to the lioness. Then she waved to a lion a few yards away on a high rock in the large enclosure. "And that's M'Bari. They're the only two in this part of the zoo. They've been mates for years and love each other very much, don't you Etosha?"

M'Bari lifted his head and roared. Charon understood him to say, "This is my territory. It belongs to me, M'Bari."

"Don't worry, M'Bari," Charon said aloud. "We don't want to encroach upon your territory."

The lion looked directly at Charon but said nothing more.

"That's exactly what he's trying to say," the second zookeeper—a man named Derek—said with a smile. "In fact, I need to warn you all that you're now in the spray zone."

"What does that mean?" Matilda asked.

"M'Bari likes to assert his claim to the territory by urinating on people who get too close," Derek explained.

Johnny made a face of disgust. "Gross."

Molly turned to Etosha and motioned with her hand. Etosha followed her along the fence and then pressed her body against the fence as Molly stroked her through the chain.

"You see how I did that, Johnny?" Molly said, still stroking the beast. "I'll do it again, but this time, you stand beside me and pet her, okay?"

"Okay." Johnny took a few steps to stand beside Molly.

Matilda held her phone in front of her, saying she would capture the encounter on video. Charon wasn't sure what she meant.

Derek handed Molly some meat, and Molly fed it to the lioness through the fence as she said, "Good, girl."

Then Molly made the same motion with her hand. Etosha followed her along the fence, turned and pressed her flank against it, and Johnny touched her fur with his bare hand. He stroked her a few more times before Etosha returned to the spot where she expected to be fed.

Molly gave her another piece of meat and repeated, "Good, girl."

"Is there any way I could pet M'Bari?" Johnny asked.

"Only if he comes over of his own accord," Derek explained. "And he may. Let's watch and see."

"Come on, M'Bari," Charon said. "Let Johnny stroke your mane, won't you?"

The zookeepers seemed surprised when M'Bari stepped down from his rock and came to the fence. First, he licked the lioness's head a few times, and then he walked around her to press his flank against the fence in front of Molly and Johnny.

Johnny stroked the lion's mane and fur. "Thank you, M'Bari. I've always wanted to pet a lion. I can't believe I'm doing it."

Without warning, the lion turned his backside to the fence and sprayed Johnny with piss.

The crowd laughed.

"Oh, no!" Matilda said. "Are you alright?"

"Thanks a lot, M'Bari," Johnny said, though he didn't seem angry. "I thought we were friends."

M'Bari turned and pressed his other flank against the fence, inviting Johnny to pet him again.

Johnny went to the fence and stroked the lion's fur. "I wish I could go inside the enclosure."

"I'm afraid we can't let you do that," Molly said.

"Why not?" Johnny asked.

"It's too dangerous," Derek said. "They've had some training and human interaction, but they're still dangerous predators that could kill you."

Johnny turned to Charon and shrugged. "Like that matters."

There was an awkward silence before Matilda said, "Thank you both so much for giving Johnny this opportunity."

"Yeah, thanks," Johnny said. "I guess now I need a shower."

A few of the spectators laughed again.

Molly unlatched the gate for them to exit. "It was our pleasure."

As they left the exhibit, Matilda asked Johnny, "Don't you want to clean up in the bathroom, so we can see the rest of the zoo?"

"I'm too tired," Johnny replied.

"They have a tram tour," she said. "Would you like to do that?"

"I think I want to go lie down, if that's okay," the boy said.

Matilda gave Charon a worried glance. "Of course, it is."

* * *

Although the plan had been for Matilda to drive the three of them the two-hour trip back to Los Angeles after a day at the zoo, Johnny's condition proved worrisome, and both Matilda and Charon agreed they should wait and make the drive in the morning. So, Charon secured rooms at a nearby hotel, and, while Johnny showered and rested, Charon and Matilda went down to a bistro on the main floor of the hotel to lunch.

"He's so much weaker than when I last saw you in Vegas," Matilda said as they sat across from one another at a small table near a window.

"The parade in New Orleans was hard on him," Charon said. "He never recovered."

102

"Poor thing," she said. "I've missed him." Then she added, "And you."

Charon reached across the table and squeezed Matilda's hand. He wished, more than anything, that he had the courage to tell her who he was. He knew she cared for him, and he didn't want to leave without an explanation.

"You're the only person I know from our generation who doesn't own a cell phone," she teased. "I found myself wanting to call you, you know."

They ordered sandwiches and tea from the waitress, and then Charon asked, "Have you had any luck locating Johnny's sister?"

Her face transformed with her lovely smile. "Yes, as a matter of fact. I've narrowed it down to a neighborhood in South Los Angeles."

Charon raised his brows. "That's good work, Matilda. Do you think you'll find her, then?"

"I do," she said, still smiling. "I was hoping you'd come with me. We could go after we take Johnny back to the hospital in the morning."

"I would like that."

Their food arrived, so Charon watched as Matilda cut her sandwich into bite-size pieces. Then he said, "I wanted to ask you about something else."

Suddenly, Charon was bombarded by her unwitting prayer: *Please ask me out. Please ask me out.* Aloud, she asked, rather nonchalantly, "What is it?"

Charon fought the smile wanting to cross his face. "About Johnny. I think he feels like he hasn't served a purpose, and I wondered if we might help him find one. And maybe if he did something kind and helpful, he'd feel better about himself."

Matilda frowned. "We don't have much time. Do you have an idea?"

Charon took a sip of his tea. "He told me what he went through in the foster system, how his foster families didn't accept and support him because he's gay."

"I'm surprised he shared that with you. Did he tell you about the fire?"

Charon nodded.

"Wow. I'm impressed. He must be very fond of you."

"As I am of him."

"So, do you have something in mind?" she asked.

"I think he ought to share his story, to help other children like him know they aren't alone," he said. "And maybe he could have an impact on how foster children are placed."

"That's actually a good idea. We could make a video and load it up on Youtube."

He had no idea what that meant. "Can you help with that?"

"Easily," she said. "If Johnny feels up to it, we can do it tonight."

They were quiet for a while as they ate. He delighted in watching her.

When she noticed him watching her, she said, "Are you laughing at me? At the way I cut up my sandwich?"

"No, I..."

"I like to eat all my food this way—even my pizza. I don't like biting from a larger piece and feeling bits of food falling to my plate. This is simpler. I suppose I'm a simple person."

He laughed—a hard laugh. "I dare say, there's nothing simple about you, Matilda."

When they'd finished their lunch, they ordered another sandwich to-go and, after it arrived, headed back up to the rooms, where they found Johnny napping. They left his lunch on the side table and went to Matilda's room next door, so as not to disturb him.

Matilda sat on one of the beds. Charon took the upholstered chair across the room from her, near the window.

"I haven't been able to stop thinking about you," Matilda said without looking at him.

"There's something I need to tell you." His heart raced. He'd been dreading this conversation.

"Oh, God. Don't tell me you're married."

"No."

"That's a relief."

It was a good thing he was sitting across the room from her. If he'd been closer, he would have taken her into his arms and avoided the subject. But he had to tell her. He couldn't let it go any longer. "I won't be staying. I have to return home."

"When?"

"I'm not sure, but soon, I think."

"Where's home?"

He averted his eyes. "You won't have heard of it."

"Your father said you were Greek."

"That's right."

She wiped a tear from her cheek. "That's a shame. Because, you see, I've never met anyone like you."

"Nor I you."

She stood and crossed the room to him, kneeling on the floor at his feet. She put her hands on his knees, sending shocks of electricity up his limbs to his core. "Charon, why can't we try to make a go of this...*thing* between us? If the distance makes it too hard, we'll break it off. But don't we both deserve a try?"

He cupped her chin. "Beautiful Matilda. I'd like nothing more than to make a go of it with you."

"Then what's stopping you?"

"Once I leave, I don't think I'll ever come back."

"Not even to see me?"

"I won't be able to."

"Then, I'll come see you."

He gave a sad, half smile. "I'm afraid that's not possible."

Tears flooded her eyes. He couldn't resist leaning over and brushing his mouth across her sweet lips.

When he pulled away, she looked up at him and said, "Anything's possible, if you want it badly enough."

He wiped her tears with his thumbs. "Why don't we check on the boy and talk more about this later?"

"I don't like leaving things this way. I want to know where we stand."

"I'm falling in love with you, Matilda. I don't think I'll ever meet someone like you again."

She wrapped her arms around his waist and pressed her cheek against his belly. Heat surged through him.

"I feel the same way about you," she said into his shirt. "And now I'm more determined than ever to make a go of it."

He held her and sighed. If only such a thing were possible.

* * *

That evening, Matilda and Charon convinced Johnny to make a video about his experiences in the foster care system. Matilda told him there was no need to talk about the fire or juvie, but Johnny insisted they were part of his story.

Charon watched on as Matilda pointed her phone at Johnny, who sat up on the hotel bed and told his story. He included more details Charon hadn't heard—such as how one foster brother had physically beaten him.

It took everything Charon had not to break down and cry.

While Matilda edited the video, on something called a "laptop," which she had to get from the trunk of her car, Charon took Johnny for a walk, so the boy could get some fresh air.

"Why a lion?' Charon asked him as they turned a corner.

"I don't know." Then he said, "I guess because they're so powerful. Even the one in the zoo had *some* control over himself and his surroundings. Maybe I admire that."

"That's a profound thought for a sixteen-year-old mortal," Charon said.

"I wish I could have gone into the enclosure," Johnny added. "In my mind, I always saw myself petting a lion with nothing between us."

"I'm sorry you're disappointed."

"Oh, God. I don't mean to sound ungrateful. I can't tell you how much all of this has meant to me—the video idea, too. I'm happier than I've been in a very long time."

"Did Matilda tell you she's close to finding your sister?"

"Yeah, she did. I'm trying not to get my hopes up."

"Tell me more about her," Charon said.

"She loves animals," he said. "She would have loved the zoo today. And she loves all kinds—even ugly ones, like snakes and rats. She's not afraid, not of bugs or anything."

"You admire your sister," Charon observed.

"She can also draw. She has a real knack for drawing animals. I once told her she should do portraits of people's pets. There could be money in that."

Charon said, "She's brave and talented."

"And cute as can be, especially when she smiles. Most little sisters get on your nerves, but not mine—not usually. She was all I ever had."

Charon could see the boy's eyes filling with tears.

"But that's not true anymore, is it, Johnny? You have me. And you have Matilda."

Johnny nodded.

They'd circled the block and were only a few yards away from the hotel.

"You're not alone, okay?" Charon said.

Johnny was quiet as they took the elevator up to the room.

"Did you have a nice walk?" Matilda asked from where she sat in Charon and Johnny's room at the desk with her laptop computer.

Johnny plopped down on his bed. "Yeah. It felt good to get out."

"I'll order a pizza," Matilda said. "Does that sound okay?"

"Can you get it with Canadian bacon and mushrooms?"

"Whatever you want," Matilda said. "That okay with you, Charon?"

"I'm not hungry, so don't worry about me."

"How's the video?" Johnny asked.

"I'm all done editing. It's uploading to Youtube now. Why don't we watch it together once the pizza gets here?"

"What if no one sees it?" Johnny asked.

"Oh, people will see it," Matilda said. "Not only did I stuff the description with all the right keywords, but Charon is paying for views."

Charon didn't really know what it all meant, but he trusted Matilda. "Your message *will be heard*. Don't you worry about that."

"I'm sure you'll make a difference," Matilda added.

Johnny smiled. "At least I won't be around for the backlash and the hate comments from trolls."

"Trolls?" Charon had always believed them to be mythical creatures.

"They're the worst," Johnny said. "Avoid them at all costs."

Charon gave Matilda a quizzical look, causing Johnny to bust out laughing. His laughter was contagious. Charon didn't know why they were all in hysterics, but he enjoyed it tremendously.

* * *

That night, after they'd watched the video and Matilda had gone to her room, Charon and Johnny readied for bed.

Before they'd turned off the lamps, Johnny asked, "Will you be there to meet me when I go?"

"At the gates of Hades?" Charon asked.

109

Johnny nodded. "It would be nice to know I'll see a friendly face."

Charon had already explained to Johnny why he was here, so he just said, "If Hades will allow it, I'll do everything in my power to be there."

"Who would it be, if not you?" Johnny asked.

"Probably Hermes. Have you heard of him?"

"I think so. But I'd like it to be you."

Charon took a deep breath. "I'll be there, then. Whatever it takes, I'll be there for you, Johnny. I promise."

"Thanks, man."

Charon had an idea for distracting the boy from his morbid thoughts. "How would you like to visit M'Bari and Etosha tonight?"

"Isn't the zoo closed?"

Charon smiled. "I could take you *inside* the enclosure, if you're willing to god-travel."

Johnny sat up in his bed. "What's god-travel?"

"It's a way to travel *through* space rather than *across* it. It's faster than flight or chariot."

"What does it feel like?" Johnny asked.

"There's pressure all around you, like you're being squashed by the Hydra, but it's brief."

"I wonder if it's like apparating in *Harry Potter*."

"I wouldn't know," Charon said.

"It doesn't matter. I want to do it." Johnny stood up. "Can we go right now?"

"If you're feeling up to it."

"I am."

Charon slipped on his shoes. Johnny did the same.

"A few rules first," Charon said. "I can't travel you in and out without holding your hand. You must hold on the entire time."

Johnny smiled. "I suppose I can handle that."

Charon blushed. "I won't be able to get you out of there if you let go. A lion can strike in less than a second."

"I won't let go."

"You must also promise to keep this between us. No videos about it. No telling Matilda. Agreed?"

"Agreed."

"And finally, don't cause trouble for the lions. We're intruding on *their* home, so we must be respectful. I don't want to hurt them. Understood?"

"Understood."

* * *

Charon held tightly to Johnny's hand as they god-traveled from the hotel room in San Diego to the lion enclosure at the Elephant Odyssey Exhibit. Most of the animals were sleeping, but not all. Etosha sat on her haunches as M'Bari licked her ear. Charon and Johnny hadn't been standing in the far corner on a large boulder of the enclosure for long when the lions jumped to their feet and sniffed the air.

"M'Bari," Charon said. "We returned for a visit. May we approach you?"

The lion growled. "You're intruding."

"Maybe I can do something for you in exchange for a favor," Charon said. "You see, I'm a god. I have the ability to grant wishes."

"Take me back to Africa," M'Bari said.

"I don't want to go back," Etosha growled.

"They seem angry," Johnny said, not understanding their talk. "Maybe this wasn't a good idea."

"You don't want to remain here, prisoners, forever," M'Bari said to Etosha.

111

"Not prisoners," she growled. "Beloved friends. We don't have to fight for our food. We're safe."

"Safe, but not free," M'Bari howled.

"Will you go without me?" Etosha asked.

"No."

Johnny repeated, "Maybe this wasn't a good idea."

Etosha whined, "Let's go to Africa together, then."

Charon stepped forward. "Let my friend pet you without the fence between us, and I'll take you there."

"How can we trust you?" Etosha whined.

"Take us first," M'Bari growled.

"Stand with us on this rock, and I'll do it," Charon said.

Slowly, the two lions approached them.

"What's going on?" Johnny whispered.

"Hold very still," Charon replied. "We're taking the lions back to Africa."

Johnny's face turned whiter than Charon had ever seen it as the lions stepped beside them on the boulder. Charon god-traveled the entire boulder, and all four of them on it, to the middle of the African savannah, where it was early morning.

The two lions leaped from the boulder and ran into the high grass, shrieking with pleasure.

"Don't forget our deal!" Charon called out, losing sight of the beasts.

Then, in the distance, he saw them running toward him and the boy. Perhaps the lions meant to make a meal out of them, after all. Before Charon could god-travel them to safety, Johnny broke loose of his hand and began to run in the direction of M'Bari and Etosha.

Charon and M'Bari reached Johnny at the same time. The lion bolted into the air and slammed Johnny down to the ground. Charon fell onto the back of the beast, intending to throw him off the boy, but as he wrapped his arms around the lion, Charon realized the beast was licking Johnny's face. And Johnny was laughing!

Thank you, Charon! Johnny prayed. *This is the most amazing moment of my life!*

Chapter 11

Back in Los Angeles, Charon and Matilda left the hospital, where Johnny was resting, to perform the final location spell in search of Jessie. Matilda drove them to South Los Angeles. She parked at a Subway Restaurant on S. Vermont Ave.

They went inside and ordered sandwiches—even though Charon wasn't hungry, he ordered one, too—before sitting in a corner booth. As Matilda cut her sandwich into bite-size pieces, she caught him up on her progress.

He studied her as she explained all she'd done. He found he was distracted by the idea that he had to drink as much of her in as he could, since he didn't know how much longer he'd be in her company.

"So, you see, I printed out a map from Google of the ten blocks I got from the last location spell," she said, pulling a folded piece of paper from her bag and flattening it on the table. "I just need to perform a dowsing spell to find the exact location."

From her bag, she pulled out a teardrop pendant dangling from the end of a silver chain. The pendant was engraved with a sigil shaped like one-half of a clam shell. Matilda held the pendant over the map and let it dangle from its chain. As she rotated it clockwise, she said, "Please show me the location of Johnny Trevino's sister, Jessica."

Charon and Matilda leaned over the map, their heads close, as they watched the pendant swing for several rounds before it began to slow down and come to a stop. The tip of the teardrop pendant pointed to a large building on the map.

Matilda read, "John Muir High School." She looked up excitedly. "It's across the street, less than a block away!"

"But there must be hundreds of students at that school," Charon said. "And we don't know her last name. How will we find her?"

"We could wait for school to end and try another spell, one where the smoke leads you to the lost person."

"You can do that?" he asked.

"Ye of little faith," she teased.

He resisted the urge to lean across the table and kiss her. "Why don't we invite Johnny to join us?"

"Good idea. It might be his only chance to see her, if the foster family won't cooperate. They sometimes don't, you know."

They finished their sandwiches and then drove to the hospital to see Johnny. When Charon attempted to follow Matilda into Johnny's room, he found himself unable to enter. He looked above the door frame to see a piece of paper with a drawing of a symbol on it—the same sigil that had prevented him from entering Matilda's hotel apartment.

"What's this?" Charon pointed to the symbol.

"A protective ward," Matilda said, returning to the hallway to look up at her handy work. "It prevents anything nonhuman from entering."

"It won't keep out Thanatos, you realize," Charon said softly, so no one would overhear. "Nothing can stop Death."

She narrowed her eyes at him. "What makes you so sure?"

"I'm going downstairs for some coffee. Want some?"

"No thanks," she said.

Once Matilda had returned to Johnny's room, Charon removed the paper containing the sigil. It burned his hand, so he dropped it on the floor. If Matilda were to notice it, perhaps she'd suspect it had fallen on its own.

As he took the elevator to the coffee vending machine on the first floor, he prayed to Thanatos, asking if he knew how much time Johnny had left.

Two days, Thanatos replied, telepathically.

Tears pricked Charon's eyes as he stepped from the elevator toward the snack room and vending machines. It seemed impossible that someone he'd grown to care for so deeply would be gone in so little time.

I want to be the one to take him through, Charon prayed to Than. *When you come for him, take me, too.*

When Charon slipped his dollars into the coffee machine, he noticed Thanatos standing in a corner beside the machine. Charon looked around and was glad that the only other person in the room was on his way out.

"Are you sure you're ready to come home?" Than asked.

"I suppose I am." Charon pushed the button to dispense his cup of coffee.

"What of Matilda, the necromancer?" Thanatos asked.

Charon gave Than a sharp, suspicious look. "How did you know that about her?" Then it occurred to him. "You set me up, didn't you? You meant for us to meet."

"She's been a thorn in my side for years," Than said.

"Has she ever succeeded in bringing someone back?"

116

"No, but not because she hasn't tried dozens of times," Than replied. "I was hoping you'd talk some sense into her."

"I'm sorry I haven't been any help to you," Charon said with too much sarcasm.

"Don't be angry with me," Thanatos said.

"I'm not angry. Just frustrated."

"Maybe Zeus would agree to make her one of us," Than put in.

"He wouldn't. I know he wouldn't. Unless..."

"Unless what?" Than asked.

Charon held his tongue.

Thanatos crossed his arms. "My grandmother Demeter knows another way, but it's very painful."

Charon lifted his brows. "I'm listening."

"You rub ambrosia on every inch of the mortal's skin," Than explained. "And then you set the mortal on fire and burn them alive."

The ferryman shuddered. "Who in his right mind would ever do that?"

"The mortal body has to die so that the immortal one can rise from the ashes," Than said.

"Goodbye, Thanatos." Charon turned and left for the elevator.

When he reached Johnny's room, Charon noticed that the paper with the sigil still lay on the floor of the hall. He went inside just as Johnny was agreeing to go to the school to find Jessie.

"We should go now," Matilda said to Charon. "I would imagine the school lets out between three and four o'clock."

"Are you ready for this?" Charon asked Johnny.

The boy climbed from his bed. "Never readier."

* * *

Charon rode in the passenger seat of Matilda's car as she drove him and Johnny to the high school in South Los Angeles. The street in front of the school was lined with vehicles, each with a parent waiting to pick up students. In front of the long line were five school busses. There didn't seem to be a way into the school parking lot.

"We can't risk waiting too long," Matilda said. "If Jessie's one of the first kids out, we'll miss her."

"Park across the street," Johnny said. "We can walk, can't we?"

"Are you sure you're up for that?" Charon asked him.

"I'm sure," the boy said.

Matilda pulled into the parking lot of a barber shop across the street and parked the car. On a piece of paper, she wrote: *Johnny Trevino's sister, Jessica.* Beside the words, she drew the same clam-shell-shaped sigil he'd seen engraved on her teardrop pendant. She dropped the paper into a small silver dish and flicked her lighter until the paper caught fire. To the fire, she added a pinch of salt and a squirt of honey from a bottle.

"Now what?" Charon asked as he watched the paper burn.

"Once the paper is ash and there are no more embers," Matilda began, "the smoke should lead us to Johnny's sister."

Johnny leaned over the front seat to watch. After a few minutes, he asked, "Is it working yet?"

Matilda opened her car door. "Come on."

The three of them climbed from the car and followed the stream of smoke, which rose from the silver dish Matilda carried in front of her. The smoke curled across the street toward the school, so they followed, as soon as the traffic allowed.

Once they were across the street and standing in front of the school, Johnny stopped to catch his breath.

"Are you okay?" Matilda asked him.

He coughed several times, until blood appeared in his hand. He quickly wiped it on his sweat pants and said, "I'm fine. Let's go."

The smoke floated above the heads of the many students outside. Some stood or sat on benches, waiting to be picked up. Others walked alone or in groups down the sidewalks in different directions. And even others headed for their own cars parked in a lot on the side of the school. To Charon, the spell seemed hopeless. There were too many people around.

After hovering over the courtyard, the smoke curled toward the front door of the school, so they followed it inside.

They were accosted by a large group eager to exit. Charon flattened against the wall, along with Matilda and Johnny, to make room for the kids, who were talking excitedly among themselves and seemed oblivious to the fact that they'd nearly run over three people.

Charon made to continue into the school when Matilda said, "Wait. It's changing direction."

"I *thought* that was her!" Johnny cried, rushing from the building.

Charon and Matilda hastened after Johnny, following the line of smoke. It hovered over a girl with Johnny's coloring as she climbed into one of the vehicles, a tan sportscar, parked along the curb.

"She's leaving!" Johnny shouted as he ran toward the car.

The car pulled away before he'd reached it.

"Charon, do something!" Johnny said desperately.

Charon looked from Matilda to Johnny, wondering what he should do.

"I'm sorry, Johnny," Matilda said. "But we'll find her again, I promise."

"Give me your keys," Charon said to Matilda. "I'll bring the car around."

"Wouldn't it be just as fast if we all go?" she asked.

"No," Johnny said. "Let him go."

Matilda handed over her keys, shrugging with a look that let them know she thought they were being ridiculous. As soon as Charon was out of her view, he god-traveled to the car. From behind the wheel, he god-traveled back with the car to the middle of the street in front of the school. He started the engine and then waved and called out to Johnny and Matilda.

Matilda jerked her head back in surprise and then followed Johnny to the car.

"I saw them turn left up ahead," Charon said as he scooted to the passenger's side. "We may be able to catch up to them after all."

"How did you get back so quickly?" Matilda asked as she climbed behind the wheel.

"I found a short cut," he lied.

Johnny giggled in the back seat. "Way to go, Charon! That's my man! Or should I say...Never mind."

"What?" Matilda turned to Johnny.

"There it is!" Johnny pointed ahead at the tan sportscar they'd seen Jessie get into back at the school.

Matilda caught up to the car at a stop sign and followed it as it made a righthand turn.

Johnny coughed again for several seconds. Charon glanced back at him and saw blood on the boy's lips.

"I'm okay," Johnny said before either of them could ask. "Just step on it, Matilda. Make us fly, if you have to."

"Yeah, right," Matilda said.

Charon rolled his eyes, wishing Johnny would stop playing with fire. When the tan sportscar pulled into the driveaway of a small house, Matilda parked along the curb.

Before she'd turned the key and taken it from the ignition, Johnny was out of the car and running across the lawn toward the sportscar in the driveaway. Charon jumped out to follow, and so did Matilda.

"Jessie!" Johnny called out as the girl was slinging her book bag over her shoulder.

The girl dropped her book bag. "Johnny?"

"What's this?" the woman who'd been driving the sportscar said. She was a short, stout woman with skin as dark as Matilda's. The apples of her cheeks each had a few freckles that were the same dark auburn color as her hair.

The brother and sister shortened the distance between them and threw their arms around one another.

"I can't believe it's you!" Jessie said again and again.

The woman who'd been driving approached Matilda and Charon and asked, "What's going on here? Is that really Jessie's brother? He wasn't supposed to find us."

"I'm sorry," Matilda said. "My name is Matilda, and this is Charon."

"We were told he was in juvie, that he was dangerous…"

"He's dying," Charon said quietly, so as not to ruin the reunion taking place a few yards away.

The woman covered her mouth and said, "Oh."

"We're so sorry to barge in on you like this," Matilda said. "We just wanted Johnny to have a chance to say goodbye to his sister."

"I see," the woman said, her face paling. "How long does he have?"

"Two days," Charon said, without thinking.

Matilda shot him a look. "We don't really know. It could be days, or it could be months, but he's not doing well."

The brother and sister were talking to one another as if they were the only two people on earth. They took turns asking and answering one another's questions, until Jessie asked where he was living, and Johnny said, "In a hospital."

"Why don't you all come in and sit down?" the woman offered. "I'm Jessie's mother, by the way— Tina."

"Thank you, Tina," Matilda said, following the woman inside.

Charon followed the others into a cozy living room with a big-screen television on one wall and a long sofa beneath the front picture window. Jessie asked Johnny if he'd like to see her room, so the kids went upstairs, leaving the three adults alone.

"Can I get you something to drink?" Tina offered. "Some tea or lemonade?"

"None for me, thanks," Matilda said.

"I'm fine, thank you," Charon said.

Tina offered them a seat on the sofa and then sat in an armchair near the big-screen television opposite them.

"How did you find us?" Tina asked.

"It wasn't easy," Matilda said, giving Charon an anxious glance.

"It was more luck than anything," Charon said.

"Oh?" Tina asked, waiting for an explanation.

Matilda folded her hands in her lap. "I had a feeling she was close, so we brought Johnny to the school, hoping he might recognize her."

"That is luck, then," Tina said without sounding convinced.

Jessie and Johnny returned to the living room. Jessie went directly to her mother and whispered into her ear, her long brown ponytail bobbing with her head. With his superhuman hearing, Charon heard her ask if Johnny could stay the night.

Tina glanced at Johnny and frowned. "I suppose it would be alright, since it's a Friday night and there's no school tomorrow. Just this once."

Jessie and Johnny squealed with glee and ran into each other's arms.

"What would be alright?" Matilda asked.

"Jessie wants me to spend the night," Johnny said. "It's okay, isn't it?"

"I don't know," Matilda said. "You haven't been well. It might be best..."

"This might be his only chance," Charon said gently.

Johnny's smile faded, as did Jessie's.

"*Charon*," Matilda scolded.

"He's right," Johnny said. "This might be my last chance to spend a night catching up with her. I'm staying, Matilda. If it's alright with Jessie's mom, I'm staying."

"Just this once," Tina repeated.

Matilda stood up. "Alright, then, Johnny. I'll go back to the hospital for your things and bring them to you this evening, okay?"

Johnny's smile returned. "Thanks, Matilda. I'll see you later. Bye, Charon."

Charon waved as the two siblings went back up the stairs.

Chapter 12

As Matilda drove Charon to the hotel, she said, "I took off work again tonight."

"I hope I haven't interfered with your plans."

She gave him a sideways glance. *Are you really not going to ask me out?*

Quickly, Charon added, "Would you like to go out tonight?" It seemed counterintuitive to make himself more vulnerable to a woman with whom he was falling in love, when he'd only have to leave her the next day.

He supposed it would be difficult to leave her, regardless.

She smiled as she merged the car onto the highway. "Maybe I could cook for you. Would you like to come to my place around seven?"

"You have a kitchen?"

"It's a tiny one, but I manage."

Charon was exhausted by the number of times a day that mortals consumed food. He didn't think he could eat another bite. And the sigil above her door would surely prevent him from entering. "I'd like to take you out to the cinema."

"You want to see a *movie*?" She sounded disappointed.

"You don't like the cinema?"

"It's not that. It's just..." Unwittingly, she prayed: *I want our last days together to be memorable.*

Charon's eyes widened as he wondered what she had in mind. He could think of one thing that would make their last night together memorable. Before he realized it, he was blushing.

"If you want to see a movie," she began again. "That's fine..."

"No, no, no," he insisted. "I was just trying to think of something we haven't done. We've had a lot of meals together. What's something new we could try?"

Oh, I certainly want to try something new with you, she prayed. *I was hoping it would be in my room, on my bed, just the two of us.*

Charon broke into a fit of coughing to hide his true reaction—shock and amusement. His cough turned into laughter.

"What's so funny?" she asked.

"Nothing, I..." He searched for something to say—anything. "I was just thinking of the first time we met, how I never would have believed we'd be together like this. It's like a dream."

"That's sweet." She gave him a bashful smile. "I feel the same way."

Matilda exited the highway toward the hotel, and they were both quiet for a few minutes, until Matilda said, "I'm not sure if this would interest you, but there's a benefit tonight at the Alexandria."

Her words couldn't be less cryptic. Charon didn't know what she meant by a benefit. And he also didn't know what the Alexandria was. To hide his ignorance, he asked, "What's it all about?"

She pulled into the parking garage across the street from the hotel. "It's a ball—black tie only—held by the American Cancer Society to raise money for cancer research. The tickets are five hundred dollars a person or eight hundred dollars a couple." She circled up to the third floor of the parking garage as she added, "It's much too expensive for *me*, but if it's of any interest to *you*..."

"Let's do it," he said, wondering what in Hades he was getting himself into. What did *black tie only* even mean?

"Seriously?" Her face lit up like the sky over Mount Olympus. "Oh, Charon! This will be so much fun! And we're sure to see some famous celebrities there!"

He was pleased that she was pleased.

She parked the car and turned to him, "But what will I wear? And what about you? Will you need to rent a tux?"

"Don't worry about me," he said. "I'll manage. Do you need some money to buy a new dress?"

Her jaw dropped open as she stepped from her car. "Are you serious?"

"It's only money." He climbed from the car and pulled out his wallet before handing her more of the magically appearing cash Thanatos had given him. "Is that enough?"

"More than enough. I'm not sure I should accept this."

"Why ever not?"

"Because it's a lot of money."

"It's nothing to me," he said. "If you can use it, please take it."

"Are you sure?" She bit her lip.

"It's for a good cause, right?" He followed her through the parking garage toward the elevators.

She threw her head back and looked down her nose at him as she walked. "You're making this too easy for me to justify."

"There's no justification needed. You want this to be memorable, don't you?"

She frowned just as Charon remembered that she hadn't expressed that thought aloud.

He quickly asked, "What time does the ball begin?"

She stepped into the garage elevator. "Eight o'clock. Maybe we should meet in the hotel lobby at seven-thirty? We can walk together from there."

"I like the sound of that." He followed her into the elevator, where they were alone.

As the elevator doors closed, Matilda gave him another sideways glance and prayed: *Oh, kiss me already!*

Charon jumped, as if she'd shouted at him.

"You okay?" she asked.

"I was just thinking..." He cupped her cheeks and pulled her lips to his.

"Mmmm," she said softly. "You should think more often."

* * *

Alone in his room, Charon showered and changed into fresh clothes, all the while wondering where he would rent a tux for the ball. Out of desperation, he summoned Aphrodite for help.

He was surprised when she appeared before him, in a beautiful gown, in a matter of seconds.

Before he could greet her, Ares appeared at her side, in a dashing dinner jacket, and, right on his heels, came Athena.

Was he to have the entire council from Mount Olympus in his hotel room?

"My god, Charon, you look amazing!" gray-eyed Athena said as she gazed at him through her raven bangs.

He wanted to say the same of her. Her silver gown sparkled as much as her gray eyes.

Aphrodite brought her hands to the blonde curls on her head. "I've never seen you this lovely."

"Calm down, ladies," Ares said with a snort as he stuffed his hands into his black trouser pockets. Then to Charon he said, "We're in a hurry, so make it quick."

Charon lifted his palms and shrugged. "I need help."

"We gathered that much," Ares said.

"I need something to wear to a ball," he explained. "A tux and a black tie."

"That's easy enough." Aphrodite snapped her fingers.

Charon's jeans were replaced by sharp black trousers. His shirt was replaced by a white button-down blouse, a white vest, a black tie, and a black coat. In place of his boots were black dress shoes.

He spun around, amazed by his reflection in the mirror over the desk. He looked as sharp and as handsome as Ares.

"You look perfect," Athena said.

"We must be attending the same event," Ares said. "American Cancer Society benefit?"

"Why, yes," Charon stammered. "But why..."

Aphrodite waved a hand through the air. "We always go where the most beautiful people are."

"Pity the poor mortal who's more beautiful than she," Athena said of Aphrodite.

"Indeed." Ares rubbed at his red beard. "You think *I* like to cause trouble."

"Now, now," Aphrodite said. "Let's not spoil the mood. I should like to know why *Charon* will be attending."

Charon blushed, unsure if he should reveal the truth. What if they used it against him?

"Oh," Aphrodite said with a smile. "He's in love."

"Is that wise?" Athena asked. "Apollo said you'd be returning to your duties soon."

Aphrodite turned to Athena. "The heart wants what the heart wants. Wisdom has nothing to do with it."

"What's her name?" Ares asked.

"I thought you were in a hurry, my lord," Charon said.

"Oh, do tell us," Aphrodite said. "We'll find out soon enough."

"Matilda." Charon averted his eyes. "I was hoping you could show me how to dance."

"It's quite simple, really." Ares took Aphrodite in his arms and began to dance with her around the room.

"*One*, two, three, *one*, two, three," Aphrodite sang. "Athena?"

Athena stood before Charon and placed her lovely hand on Charon's shoulder. "Shall we?"

Aphrodite sang, "*One*, two, three, *one*, two, three."

"This is the waltz," Athena explained as they maneuvered around the room together. "If nothing else, at least you can dance this one."

"Thank you," Charon said, getting the hang of it. "It's our last night together, and we'd like it to be memorable."

"I'm sure I can help with that," Aphrodite said, just before she and the others disappeared.

Startled by their abrupt departure, Charon steadied himself and checked out his reflection once more in the mirror over the desk. As he straightened his tie and tidied his thick, wavy hair, he wondered what Aphrodite had in mind. He hoped he hadn't ruined his evening with Matilda before it had even begun.

* * *

When Charon stepped from the elevator into the hotel lobby, his breath caught. Matilda was already there, waiting for him, wearing a gown as lovely as Athena and Aphrodite's.

The royal blue fabric fit her curves like a glove, from the peak of her breasts down to her knees, where it flared out and brushed the floor. Her hair, which she usually wore down and pinned back behind her ears, was now a beautiful cascade of ringlets on the crown of her head. Her eyelids and lashes were painted, making her dark eyes even more mesmerizing.

As he crossed the lobby, he began to worry that Aphrodite would be jealous and make mischief for them.

Oh, God. You're frowning, came Matilda's unwitting prayer to him.

Before he could change his expression, she asked, "Is something the matter? Is there something wrong with the way I look?"

He took both of her hands. "No. Absolutely not. You look...stunning."

"Thank you," she smiled up at him. "I got you something, for your lapel."

She held up a single white carnation on a short stem and pinned it to his coat.

"Thank you." He realized he was probably supposed to give her a flower, too. He suddenly felt awkward and ashamed that he didn't understand such customs.

"Ready?" she asked.

He held out his arm for her. The warmth of her hand around his arm sent chills along his shoulder and down his back.

"Lead the way," he said, since he didn't know where they were going.

It was cold outside, when they reached the sidewalk.

"I've forgotten my coat," Matilda said. "Maybe I should I run back up and get it."

"Take mine." He took off the black coat of his tuxedo and draped it over her shoulders, and, just for good measure, he added some extra warmth to soothe her.

"Mmm, cozy," she said. "Thanks."

Missing the feel of her touch, he draped his arm across her shoulders. She seemed pleased as she smiled up at him again.

"I hope you won't expect too much of me on the dance floor," he said. "I only know the waltz."

"That's fortunate," she said. "It's my favorite dance."

Something buzzed from inside the tiny bag that draped from her wrist. She opened the bag and took out her phone.

"It's Johnny, checking in," she said. "I took his things over to him earlier and told him to check in with me regularly. He says he's having a blast and is feeling fine."

"That's a relief."

Matilda laughed.

"What's so funny?"

"I almost feel like we're a married couple with a son." Her face turned red. "I shouldn't have said that out loud."

He wanted to say that he would have heard it, anyway, if she'd directed the thought to him; instead, he laughed and said, "If only we were. My life would be complete."

Her mouth dropped open as she stopped in the middle of the sidewalk and turned to face him. "That's a sweet thing to say. If you really feel that way, then why leave?"

"I have no choice. I have a job to do. People depend on me."

She sighed as they continued down the sidewalk.

Not far ahead, they saw a long line of people snaking along the street.

"That can't be the line to get in, can it?" she said.

"I sincerely hope not," he said. "I'd hate for you to have to wait out in the cold."

"But your jacket is so cozy. I can still feel your body heat, from when you had it on." Then she added, "Besides, it's beautiful out, now that they've put up all the Christmas lights."

She was certainly a glass-is-half-full kind of person, he thought with a grin.

If he remembered correctly, Christmas was a celebration that coincided with the winter solstice, which was still a month away. He supposed mortals enjoyed stretching their celebrations over long periods of time, as with Dia de los Muertos.

"Oh, that's not the line to get in," Matilda observed once they were closer. "Those must be spectators hoping to get a glance at the celebrities. Come on."

Charon followed Matilda into the corner building. The foyer was magnificent, with crystal chandeliers, golden drapes along the front windows, and a skylight made of stained glass. A skirted table with two well-dressed mortals was situated at the back of the grand foyer, where a small line had formed.

"This way," Matilda said.

As they waited their turn, Matilda thanked him for his coat and returned it.

A moment later, she grabbed his hands, pressed her lips close to his neck, and whispered, "Oh my God! Don't look now, but that's Jared and Jensen walking in now!"

Charon had no idea who those people were, but he was glad to see Matilda having a good time before they'd even entered the ballroom. She squeezed his hands and squealed quietly as she stole glances at the two men and their dates walking toward them.

"Good evening," Charon said.

The two men smiled and took turns shaking his hand.

Oh, my God! I can't believe this is happening! Matilda unwittingly prayed to him.

"I'm Charon and this is Matilda," Charon said. "She's a big fan of yours."

"But you aren't?" one of them teased.

"I'm sorry," Charon blushed. "I don't know who you are."

"Don't apologize," the other one said.

"Yeah, we tend to have a better time around people who don't," the first added. "I'm Jensen, by the way. This is my wife, Danneel."

"And I'm Jared. This is Genevieve."

I'm going to die! Matilda all but screamed in his head.

Charon gave her a concerned look and realized she was speaking figuratively. Then it was his turn to pay for the tickets, so they said goodbye to the celebrities and went down the hall to the King Edward Ballroom.

The ballroom was even more magnificent than the foyer. Gold and crystal chandeliers and gilded molding on white plaster walls added to the ambience of luxury and splendor. To Charon, it rivaled the beauty of the great hall on Mount Olympus.

He and Matilda hadn't been sitting at a table long when Charon spotted Ares and Aphrodite dancing together among a dozen other couples on the dancefloor. He scanned the room for Athena, when suddenly she was at his side.

Her gray eyes twinkled down at him. "Hello, Charon."

Charon could tell by the look on Matilda's face that she was surprised someone had recognized him. The prayer that followed further supported this: *Who is this? And how does she know you?*

"You must be Matilda," Athena said before Charon could reply.

Matilda raised her brows. "I'm afraid I'm at a disadvantage. Charon hasn't mentioned you to me."

"I'm not surprised," Athena said. "We're distant relatives and rarely see one another, isn't that right, Charon?"

"Yes, that's right."

"Relatives?" Matilda's face lit up. "Are you from Greece?"

"Yes," the goddess said with a half-smile. "I'm Athena."

"Like the goddess of wisdom," Matilda said.

"Oh, you've heard of her?" The half-smile became a full one.

"I pray to her nearly every day. Along with Hecate, she's one of my favorites."

Athena cocked her head to the side. "Of the two, which would you say is your very favorite?"

"Don't answer that," Charon warned.

Matilda gave him a nervous glance. "Don't be rude, Charon."

"I, only meant there's no time to lose." He stood up. "They're finally playing a waltz. Excuse us, Athena."

He led Matilda onto the dancefloor, where Aphrodite and Ares kept stealing glances their way as he concentrated on *one*, two, three, *one*, two, three...

"Do you know that couple?" Matilda asked him after a few minutes had passed.

"More of my distant relatives."

"Charon! Did you know they would be here?"

"Not until just a few hours ago."

"Why didn't you tell me? Didn't you want to introduce us?" Then she added, unwittingly, *Or, are you ashamed for them to see you with me?*

He wrinkled his brows, wondering why she would even think such a thing. "They don't really like my kind."

"Your kind?"

"My side of the family. There isn't much interaction between us."

"Oh. Why not?"

"I don't really know, to be honest. I think maybe they believe they're better than us."

"I see."

He spun her around to the other side of the dancefloor, until, suddenly, she stopped in the middle of the floor and pointed. "That's Oprah over there! I think I'm going to faint. I've always wanted to meet her."

"Then, by all means, let's introduce ourselves."

"You can't be serious."

"I'm rarely anything else."

He gave Matilda his arm and escorted her across the room.

"Which one is Oprah?" he whispered in her ear.

"The one in the white jacket."

"Excuse me, Oprah," Charon said. "May I introduce you to Matilda Whitmore? She's a medical student and a volunteer at the Children's Cancer Ward, and she's a big fan of yours."

Oprah stood up and shook Matilda's hand. "That's impressive. What led you to work with cancer patients?"

"I'm a leukemia survivor," Matilda replied. "In fact, Charon here just helped one of my patients through a crazy bucket list that took them all over the world. Isn't that right, Charon?"

"Indeed."

"Is that so?" Oprah said. "Then there's someone I want you to meet." Oprah looked around the table and asked the woman next to her, "Where did Ellen go? She needs to have this couple on her show."

The woman beside her shrugged, but then Oprah waved to a woman across the room and shouted, "Ellen! Come here, Ellen!"

Matilda leaned against Charon. "I really *am* going to faint. I can't believe this is happening!"

"I'm looking for Portia!" the woman named Ellen shouted. "Have you seen her?"

Oprah shrugged and turned back to Matilda. "Wait until she comes back. You really must meet. Please, come sit down."

"This must be what heaven is like," Matilda whispered to Charon as he helped her to a chair.

"Not exactly," he whispered back.

Chapter 13

After an evening of dancing and talking with celebrities, Charon had hoped to escort Matilda back to his room, but, when he led her to the grand foyer, Aphrodite caught up to them, with Ares on her heels.

"Did you think you could leave without saying goodbye?" she asked Charon.

"No, I..."

She turned to Matilda. "Hello, I'm Aphrodite. And this is my date, Ares."

"Like the god and goddess," Matilda said, beaming.

"Exactly," Ares said.

"We have a surprise for you." Aphrodite winked. "Follow us outside."

Waiting at the curb was a chariot with three white mares.

Matilda clapped her hands. "Is this for us?"

"Do you love it?" Aphrodite asked.

"Yes!" Matilda squealed. "Thank you so much! How kind!"

Ares opened the door. "Climb in."

Charon helped Matilda into the chariot and then sat beside her. When he noticed she was trembling, he took off his coat and wrapped it around her shoulders.

"Thank you." She beamed up at him.

As the driver pulled away from the curb, Charon worried there would be more to this surprise than he wished.

Matilda lay her head on his shoulder and squeezed his hand. "Isn't this romantic? The stars, the Christmas lights, the skyscrapers. What a beautiful night! If this is what snobby distant relatives are like, then I need to get me some!"

Charon laughed before he kissed her cheek. "I'm glad you're pleased."

"Pleased? That's the understatement of the year. Believe me when I say this has been the best night of my life!"

The driver turned and winked at Charon. It was Poseidon! Charon would have recognized those turquoise eyes anywhere.

"Your night's about to get even better," the god of the sea said. "Hold on!"

Charon implored the god telepathically to keep their identities and godly status a secret, but not before Poseidon had steered the chariot up into the sky.

Matilda screamed.

"She doesn't know?" Poseidon called back to Charon.

"Obviously," Charon replied.

Matilda gripped the edge of the chariot. "Know what? What the heck is happening?"

"My sincere apologies, Charon. Aphrodite didn't say."

Charon held back his rage. "Please take us back to the street and to the hotel, my lord."

The three mares darted back down to the streets of Los Angeles and stopped abruptly before the hotel.

Matilda could no longer speak. Her mouth and eyes were wide with shock and fear.

"You should do what I always do," Poseidon said.

Hypnos, the fraternal twin brother to Thanatos, appeared next to Poseidon, and Matilda fell asleep.

"Hey, Bud!" Hypnos said to Charon in his cool and confident way. Of the brothers, he was by far the more outgoing, which was ironic, since he was the god of sleep. "How's it going?" He turned to Poseidon. "You called, my lord?"

"Yes, Hypnos," Poseidon said. "Please convince this young lady here that all that transpired in my chariot was but a dream."

"No problem." He snapped his fingers and disappeared.

Matilda stirred beside Charon before yawning and stretching and opening her eyes. "Oh, my. Have I been asleep?"

Charon shot Poseidon a look of relief.

"It's been a long night," Charon said to Matilda. "Let me help you inside."

"I just had the strangest dream," she said, as he opened the door for her.

Once inside the lobby, Matilda returned Charon's coat. "Why don't you come up to my place for a while?"

He stuffed his arms through the sleeves of the black jacket, searching for an excuse, since he knew the sigil over her door would not allow it. "Let's have a drink in the bar together first."

"Good idea." She unwittingly added, *I could use some courage, anyway.*

As they entered the bar, Charon thought back to the first night he'd stepped into this establishment. He couldn't believe how much his life had changed in a matter of weeks. He left his home with nothing but disdain for humanity and with no desire to experience the Upperworld or to befriend those who peopled it. Now, as much as he missed his skiff and the quiet rivers of the Underworld, he would give anything to remain with Matilda, to have a chance at love. Maybe they could get a dog, like Bill, and one day have a son, like Johnny.

He was brought from his reverie by the bartender, who smiled at Matilda and shouted, "Tillie! Girl, do you look fine! Damn!"

"Who's that?" Charon asked her.

"Ross," she said. "Don't mind him."

They sat at a table in a quiet corner. "Why does he call you Tillie?"

"That's his nickname for me. He has a nickname for everyone."

Ross was tall, muscular, and as dark as Matilda, with stunning green eyes and short, curly hair.

"Well, well, well," Ross said, as he approached their table.

"Hello, Ross," Matilda said. "This is Charon. He's visiting from Greece. Charon, this is my co-worker, Ross."

"It's a pleasure to meet you," Ross said. "What can I get for you?"

"I'll have a glass of Chardonnay," Matilda said.

Ross shook his head.

"What's wrong?" she asked him.

"Nothing. I just can't get over how fine you look. What can I get for you, Charon?"

"A shot of whiskey, please."

"He prefers Black Velvet," Matilda added.

"I bet he does," Ross said. "I'll be right back with your drinks."

As Ross left their table, Matilda blushed, but Charon had no idea why.

"Are you feeling okay?" he asked her.

"I can't wait to take you back to my place." Matilda reached over and took Charon's hand. "I thought I might show you my childhood scrapbook, if you're interested. I know you'll be leaving soon, but I don't want you to forget me."

"I'll never forget you."

She frowned. "Will I ever see you again?"

"I'm certain of it, but not for a very long time."

"Why not?"

He didn't reply.

"I don't see why I can't visit you in Greece. I can save up and pay my own way."

How he wished he could tell her the truth, but he didn't want to risk ruining what they had together. "I wish it were possible."

"Are you sure you aren't married?"

Charon laughed. "If only it were that simple. The truth is, I'm a slave to my work. Even if you came, we'd never see one another."

"I've just realized you never told me what it is you do."

"I work on a ferry," he said. "I'm always on the boat. I hardly ever leave it."

Ross returned with their drinks. "Just wave at me when you're ready for more."

"Thank you, Ross," Charon said.

Once Ross had left again, Matilda said, "How funny."

"What?" He took a sip of the whiskey.

"Did your parents name you Charon because they knew you would work on a ferry, like the ferryman of the dead?"

Charon broke out into a fit of coughing. Once he'd recovered, he said, "I suppose they did."

"I bet you get a lot of jokes at work," she added before taking a drink of her wine.

"You'd be surprised."

143

"But now that your father has left you all that money, couldn't you quit?"

He squeezed her hand. "If I abandoned my post, I'd go mad."

"Your work is important to you. I respect that."

What he couldn't say is that he literally *would* go mad. Any god who abandoned his duties would eventually go insane, unless he found someone to switch fates with him.

The thought of switching fates reminded him of something else he wanted to say. "About your mother, Matilda."

"Please don't lecture me. Not tonight." She let go of his hand and clasped her hands in front of her.

"I just want to say that she gave up her life because she wanted you to have a chance at one."

"I know that."

"But what you're doing, you're risking that chance, don't you see? Her sacrifice will mean nothing if you kill yourself in the process."

"Give me some credit, Charon. I understand all that."

There was a buzzing sound coming from her bag. Matilda took out her phone and said, "Hello?"

Charon heard Tina, Jessie's mother, say, "We had to rush Johnny to the hospital. You should come as soon as possible."

"Okay, thank you, Tina." Matilda returned the phone to her bag.

"Johnny's not well?" Charon asked, though he already knew the answer.

"Tina's with him at the hospital."

"I'll take care of the tab, and then we can head over there, too," Charon said.

Tears filled Matilda's eyes. "I'll get us a cab."

* * *

Charon and Matilda hastened to Johnny's bedside in the children's ward of the hospital, where Jessie, Tina, and a man, who was presumably Jessie's adoptive father, were already present.

"Johnny?" Matilda asked.

He wore a breathing tube, and each labored breath rustled like harsh wind through heavy sticks. He opened his eyes and looked at Matilda, but he didn't speak.

"I'm Craig, Jessie's father," the other man in the room said to Charon and Matilda. He was short and round, like his wife, and darker skinned. His head was slick and his face beardless. "Why don't we have a word out in the hall?"

"You go," Charon said to Matilda. "I want to stay with him."

As Matilda followed Craig to the hall, Charon took Johnny's hand. "I'll be with the whole way. You can count on me."

Johnny blinked his understanding and prayed: *Don't let go of my hand.*

Jessie broke into tears. From the look of her, it wasn't the first time. The girl's eyes were swollen and red as she fell against her mother.

"I'm sorry, my love," Tina whispered.

Out in the hall, Craig was updating Matilda on Johnny's condition. Charon could hear every word, but he didn't need to. He already knew from Thanatos that Johnny would die today.

Suddenly a force, like a typhoon, pushed Charon from the room and out into the hallway, where Matilda was re-taping her sigil over the door.

When he flew past her, she asked, "Charon? What's going on?"

"I told you, nothing can stop Death."

"Come on, pal," Craig said. "There's no need to be harsh."

"I need to hold his hand," Charon said as tears pricked his eyes. "Take that thing down, so I can hold his hand."

Matilda cupped his cheeks. "What's gotten into you?"

From inside the room, Tina shouted, "We're losing him! Call the doctor!"

Charon looked inside the room and saw Thanatos leaning over Johnny. Matilda rushed to Johnny's side and took his hand. Craig shouted for a doctor.

However hard he tried to get to Johnny's side, Charon was prevented by the force of the sigil.

"We love you, Johnny!" Matilda cried as tears slipped down her cheeks. "Wait for me in heaven, okay? And say hello to my mother, and to yours."

Matilda kissed Johnny's cheek as he took his final breath and Thanatos lifted the boy's soul from its body.

I'm going with you, Charon reminded Thanatos from the hallway as the doctor and Craig rushed past him. He supposed there was no way to say goodbye to Matilda. He couldn't get to her side, and he couldn't possibly say goodbye from the hall.

It was time to go.

He god-traveled with Than and Johnny's soul to the gates of the Underworld, where Hermes met them on Charon's skiff.

"It's about time!" Hermes shouted with glee. "I've never been so happy to see someone as I am you, Charon."

"I'll take over from here," he said to Hermes.

Charon took his pole and led the skiff past Cerberus, through the gates, and to the Room of Judgment. It was no surprise that Johnny was sentenced to the Elysian Fields.

"There's something you need to know," Charon said to Johnny.

The soul of Johnny was in a daze, as were all who boarded. His short, miserable life passed before Charon's eyes. For the first time, the experience made Charon sob.

"Don't worry, Johnny," Charon said kindly. "The Lethe River helps you to forget your former life. In the Fields of Elysium, you'll have a happy, wonderful afterlife, filled with the shared delusions of all who dwell there. But you won't remember me. So, this is goodbye, my friend."

Johnny had already forgotten. He looked over the fields with the smile of ignorance and whispered, "How beautiful."

Chapter 14

Over the next few months, Charon bore his duties gravely. As he read the memories of the souls that boarded his ferry day after day, he never felt more compassion, sorrow, or pity. He spoke words of comfort to his passengers. He felt more deeply than he used to feel in the old days, before his quest.

And he never stopped thinking of Matilda. She prayed to him daily, though she did not know it. She asked him why he'd left without saying goodbye. She imagined Johnny's death had been too painful for Charon to stay. She speculated that she was a reminder of the loss, and that it must have been easier for Charon to run away from it all. She imagined that he only wanted to return to Greece and to forget.

But he'd never forget.

Although they brought him pain, her prayers kept him going. It had been centuries since anyone had prayed to him. It was nice to know that someone in the world was thinking of him.

Hades had been pleased by the results of Charon's adventures, though he had no knowledge of Charon's broken heart. Apollo, too, had confirmed that the ferryman's life was no longer in danger, because he had become more than a mere spectator to his souls. Charon shared in their pain and sorrow. Because he understood what it was to be mortal, and because he truly felt what they felt, he was no longer a passive receptacle that aged with each memory; instead, he was an active participant in life.

Despite the success of his quest, Charon wasn't convinced that he was better off than he'd been before he left the Underworld. At least, then, he hadn't known what he'd been missing. Now, he could only think of Matilda.

He longed for her, and it was driving him mad.

When he could hardly bear the longing, he took his skiff to the Elysian Fields to look for Bill and Johnny. They no longer recognized Charon. The Lethe, the River of Forgetfulness, had washed away their memories; but, Charon did remember, and it comforted him to see them. The two souls were often frolicking in the fields together, though they had no knowledge that they'd both been cherished by the ferryman of the Underworld.

Sometime after Persephone had left with Hecate and her familiars to join the Olympians for the spring and summer, Charon sensed something strange and foreboding near the gates.

Cerberus's howling confirmed Charon's suspicion that something was amiss.

The ferryman directed his boat to the entrance, where the Acheron met the Styx. A blazing sphere outside the gates nearly blinded him. Once his eyes had adjusted, he was shocked to find Matilda amidst the blazing light.

And Matilda was shrieking in pain.

She held a blade that was covered in blood. Whether the blood belonged to her, he did not know. At her feet lay ashes, blood, and the horns of a ram. He now feared that she'd resorted to black magic, which required the sacrifice of another living being.

He hastened toward the gates and cried out to her.

As he reached the blazing sphere, he found he could not penetrate the light to get to her, to help her, and to end her agony. Her screams filled *him* with agony, too, but he was helpless as he watched her cut herself with the dripping blade.

Around her feet were a series of concentric sigils connecting into a larger circle that expanded the perimeter of the blazing sphere. From some of these symbols, a putrid, disgusting odor rose and carried through the gates. Charon realized there was magic in the odor—that it was the means by which Matilda would breach the gates and find her way to her dead mother's soul.

No wonder she had waited for Persephone and Hecate to leave the Underworld. Although Hades, Thanatos, and the Furies were powerful enough to defend the realm, the goddess of witches would have sensed the spellcaster long before now. Matilda never would have made it this far with Hecate at home.

And now it may be too late for Charon to save her.

"Monique Johnson, I call thee from the dead!" Matilda screamed. "Monique Johnson, I call thee from the dead!"

From the depths of the Phlegethon, the abomination of an untethered soul floated toward him. It was the soul of Matilda's mother, the one who'd switched fates with her daughter five years ago.

Charon remembered her now. He'd seen the girl and her mother in a wall of fire. He'd seen Matilda, and she'd seen him.

She hadn't been lying when he'd first met her at the bar, and she'd said she'd seen him somewhere before. She hadn't been able to recall where it had been because her mortal mind couldn't acknowledge the truth.

Now, Cerberus's howls had, at last, brought their master to the gates.

"What's this?" Hades demanded.

"A mistake!" Charon shouted from outside the gates. "Please give me a chance to rectify it!"

Hades said nothing as Charon turned once more to the blazing sphere and shouted Matilda's name.

But again, she screamed, "Monique Johnson, I call thee from the dead!"

"Look at me!" Charon cried to her. "You must stop this! You won't survive!"

"Monique Johnson, I call thee from the dead!"

The soul of Matilda's mother floated closer to the gates.

"It's *me*, Matilda! It's Charon! *Your* Charon! Please, look at me!"

Finally, Matilda peered through the blinding light and met his gaze. Her mouth dropped open with recognition.

"Charon? Is that really *you*?"

Tears of relief fell from his eyes. "Believe me when I say you won't survive this if you don't stop this now!"

The soul of Matilda's mother hovered near the gates, moving neither forward nor backward.

"You better put a stop to this!" Hades warned him. "I'll have to take both souls. I'll have no choice."

"Please, Matilda!" Charon shouted. "Trust me, and do as I say. Stop this spell. You can never trust black magic. There are always consequences, and never good ones. The only way your mother will leave this realm is if you take her place."

"I *will* take her place, if it means I can be with *you*!"

Charon shook his head. "You don't understand. Mortal souls...they have no memory, no will of their own. You wouldn't be *you*."

"You're right. I *don't* understand!"

"Trust me. Will you do that?"

With eyes full of tears and with blood dripping from her wrist, she nodded. She covered the bleeding wrist with a trembling hand. "I miss you more than I expected to!"

"I miss you, too. I'm sorry I left without saying goodbye."

"I understand now. You wanted to bring Johnny here. Isn't that right?"

"Yes. I made a promise to him. Your protective ward kept me from the room. I couldn't get to you to say goodbye. I'm sorry." He wiped the tears from his eyes. "But I hear your prayers, Matilda. They bring me pain and comfort."

"You can hear me?"

"When you direct your thoughts to me, yes."

"Then you know how I feel."

"I do. And I feel the same way about you."

"She's running out of time," Hades warned.

"You have to stop, Matilda!" Charon pleaded. "Put an end to it now!"

"Goodbye, my love!" she cried just before she snuffed out the candle at her feet and disappeared from his sight.

The soul of her mother was instantly sucked back into the depths of the Phlegethon and carried to the Elysian Fields, where it belonged.

Charon took a deep breath and sighed.

"That was close," Hades said, before he, too, vanished.

Charon, exhausted and overcome with relief and remorse, fell in a heap in the middle of his boat and sobbed until the next soul called to him.

     * * *

After that near-disaster, Matilda's prayers to Charon changed. They were no longer unwitting prayers, but ones spoken consciously, like one half of a conversation. She spoke to him as soon as she woke up each morning.

For example, she'd say: *Good morning, Charon! It looks like it's going to rain today, but I suspect it never rains where you are.*

Later, in the middle of class, she'd pray: *If only you could whisper the correct answer to me, I might have a chance at passing this test.* And, at lunch, she'd say: *Yes, I'm cutting my sandwich into bite-size pieces. Don't judge.*

In the afternoons, she'd tell him about the patients in the children's ward. There was a new boy named Victor who reminded her of Johnny.

In the evenings, while she tended bar, she'd complain about her aching feet: *You're a god. Can't you do something to help my aches and pains?*

And, once, she made him bust out laughing when she said: *There's a really hot guy hitting on me tonight. Don't you want to come and defend your territory? You could piss on him, like M'Bari!*

At bedtime, she would say: *I'm imagining you next to me, Charon. I can almost feel your breath. If you were here beside me, this is what I'd do to you...*

Sometimes Thanatos would catch Charon smiling or even laughing out loud. When the god of death asked what was so funny, Charon would shake his head and say, "Nothing. Never mind."

Matilda also seemed to have finally come to terms with her mother's death, which was evident when she said: *Tell my mom I said hello*; or sometimes:

Tell my mom I'm thinking of her; and, most often: *Tell my mom I miss her.*

Although he couldn't answer her back, he was uplifted by her devotion to him. Her constant prayers lightened his burden. He found it easier to share in the sorrows of his passengers when Matilda's sweet voice supplied him with happier thoughts.

One day, as Thanatos boarded the skiff with two souls from India, the god of death said, "By the way, I never thanked you for solving my problem with the necromancer."

Charon pulled his pole through the Acheron. "I didn't do it for you."

"Even so," Than said. "I want to express my gratitude."

Charon said no more to the god of death, because he was soon preoccupied with Matilda's prayers about a girl whose cancer was in remission.

Charon even composed a poem, which he often sang to himself: *Matilda's voice is lovely, soft, and sweet, and it carries me through the dark and deep.*

He knew Matilda would be better off with a mortal who could be physically present in her life, but he was grateful that—for a while, anyway—she was his.

* * *

By the end of May, Matilda's prayers had changed again. She was off from school for the summer, and though she had increased her hours tending bar and volunteering at the hospital, her mind seemed less occupied and more prone to longing.

Oh, Charon! Please tell me that I'll see you one day soon, and that I won't have to die to do it!

And where her prayers to him at bedtime were once playful and sensual, such as, *I'm imagining you touching me here and here...*They were now tinged with desperation: *I need you, Charon! I can't take this anymore! Please find a way back to me!*

Charon found himself frowning more and more often, feeling utterly powerless to do anything about Matilda's growing despair. He was a god. Could he do nothing?

Then one day, he had an idea. He directed his skiff toward the field of asphodel. Hoping not to leave his duties too long, he left the boat on the bank of the Phlegethon and ran to the field, where he lay down and went to sleep to search the Dreamworld for Hypnos.

It didn't take long for the god of sleep to appear to him. "Charon? What are you doing here? The moon won't be full for another two weeks."

"I need a favor. Can you help me?"

"That depends on what it is."

"Take me to see Matilda, in her dreams."

"Matilda?"

"You remember the mortal you put to sleep in Poseidon's chariot, don't you?"

"How could I forget? Bud, she was hot!"

"I want to speak to her in a dream."

"No problem. Follow me."

While Charon's physical body continued to sleep in the field of asphodel, his psyche followed Hypnos through the colorful prism that bordered millions of individual dreams. Hypnos—or Hip, as the other Underworld gods frequently called him—had the responsibility of monitoring and enriching the experiences people had in their sleep.

Charon thought he caught a glimpse of Matilda up ahead. He hurried after her.

Through the colorful rays and streams of translucent violets and reds, Charon saw Matilda running down a sidewalk between two large buildings on what appeared to be a college campus.

"Matilda!" he shouted.

She disappeared behind the corner of one of the buildings, so he hurried to catch up to her. Up ahead, he saw her in a white cotton blouse and tight blue jeans. She had a book satchel over one shoulder and a loose paper in one hand. Her black curls bounced over her shoulders as she ran.

"Matilda!" he called again.

She looked back over her shoulder at him. "Charon?"

"Yes. It's me."

"Oh, thank goodness! Please help me! I can't find my class!"

"Huh?"

She ran toward him. "I'm not sure what class I'm supposed to be in, much less where it is. This schedule is gibberish. I can't even remember if I paid my tuition. What if I'm not registered anymore?"

He grabbed her hands. "Calm down. Your spring term is over, remember? You're on summer break."

"What?" Her brows formed a "v" between her beautiful, dark eyes. "No, Charon. I'm late. I'm supposed to be in class. I just don't know *which* class, or where it is! Please help me get this figured out!" She glanced at the building behind her, trying to catch her breath. "Where am I? Am I at the right campus?"

He squeezed her hands. "This is a dream. You're in bed, dreaming."

She looked up at him. The "v" between her eyes had vanished, and her mouth had dropped open. He wanted to kiss her.

"This is a dream," he said again, before he pressed his lips to hers.

Because the contact wasn't physical, it was a disappointment to Charon; but, it was certainly better than nothing.

"Oh, Charon," she purred as her hand raised to his cheek. "Is it really you?"

"I've come to tell you that I can hear your prayers. I know I should also tell you to move on, to find a man who can..."

"Don't. Don't talk like that. I'm in love with you."

He kissed her again.

"I hope I never wake up," she said in between kisses.

"I'll try to visit you in your dreams as often as I can, and I'll speak to Hypnos about these chaotic nightmares you seem to be having."

"If only I could hold you for real," she said. "Will that ever happen?"

Suddenly, she disappeared, and Charon found himself alone in the prism of streaming colors. He cried out for Hip.

The god of sleep appeared to him. "Hey, Bud. What's up?"

"She was just here," Charon said. "Where did she go? What happened?"

"She woke up, Bud. Sorry. It happens."

"Can you return her to the deep boon of sleep?"

"I'm a little busy, Charon. Sheesh. You do a guy one favor and then..."

"I'll be back at the full moon," Charon said. "Meanwhile, I'd appreciate it if you could help her have *sweet* dreams, and not those frantic ones where she can't find what she's looking for. Could you do that for me?"

"I'll see what I can do, Bud."

* * *

Two weeks later, when Charon returned to the Dreamworld at the next full moon, he solicited Hip's help in finding Matilda again. Although her dream was less chaotic, it was far from sweet.

She was sitting at a table in her room, sobbing with her face in her hands.

He touched her curly hair and whispered, "Sweet, Matilda. Don't cry."

She gasped and looked up at him. "Charon?"

He grinned. "It's me."

She jumped from her chair and threw her arms around his neck. "I'm so happy to see you. I can't tell you how much I miss you." She kissed his cheek and added, "If only I could know if this is really you. It *looks* like you! It *feels* like you! But it's probably just my imagination."

"I'm no figment," he said. "It's really me."

"But how can I be sure? Is there no way you can come to me while I'm awake?"

"I wish..."

"Could you call me? Do gods have phones?"

He chuckled. "No..."

"Could you write a letter to me and get it to me somehow, so I know I'm not just babbling on to myself?" Then she sighed and returned to the table. "Or maybe it's better that I don't know the truth. I want to believe it's you. If it's not, I don't want to know."

He squeezed her shoulders. "I'll write you a letter and ask Thanatos to deliver it."

"Thanatos? You mean Death?"

"Yes. I don't know if he'll do it, but I'll ask."

She took a deep breath and returned to his arms. "Oh, Charon. I'm miserable without you."

As much as it pained him to say it, he gently whispered, "I should let you go, then. I don't want to make you miserable. You should meet someone...a mortal."

"I'd rather be miserable and have *you* in my heart."

He kissed her just before she and her room vanished, and he was standing alone in the prism of colors.

Charon woke up in the field of asphodel and returned to his abode, where he found a pen and paper. He sat at his table and tried to work out what to say to this woman who'd come to mean so much to him.

He started over four times before he finally settled on this:

My sweet Matilda,

How I long to hold you in my arms—in my actual, physical arms rather than in the airy stuff of your dreams.

You may not remember, but you asked me to write to you, to confirm that it is I who comes to you when you sleep. Last night, and at each full moon from now on, I am yours.

If you dream of me again on a night when the moon is not full, you may be engaging with a figment in the Dreamworld and not the real me. If the moon is full, you can depend on me to be there.

I'm so proud of your excellent grades in medical school and of the progress you're making with the patients in the children's ward. Your prayers to me are heard and are more than appreciated.

In fact, your prayers keep me going. They make me laugh. They make me cry. They bring me joy and sorrow. They make me feel alive.

And please continue to tell me at night where you like to be touched.

I know I should tell you to forget about me and to move on with your life; but, I find myself incapable of doing so. If you do happen to meet someone who can give you what I can't, I'll be happy for you. You deserve to marry and to have children and to live a normal life. I want that for you...eventually.

Until then, I'm yours.

Charon

The ferryman folded the note, and, when it was time to return to his skiff to meet the souls, he handed it over to Thanatos.

"What's this?" the god of death asked.

"A letter for Matilda. Will you please deliver it to her?"

"You know what happens to mortals that come into contact me."

"Just leave it on her table in her room. Please? I'll owe you one."

"You won't owe me anything," Than replied. "I'm happy to have that necromancer off my back."

"Thank you," Charon said as tears filled his eyes. "But I do feel indebted to you for this. I'll find a way to repay you."

Charon was pleased when, later that day, Matilda's prayer to him was fervent: *I received your letter. I couldn't be happier. Thank you, thank you, thank you! I hope you'll write again!*

Matilda's prayers returned to the lighthearted, playful prayers he'd received in the early spring. He cherished them, though he couldn't help but worry over how long they would last. How soon before they would once again become tinged with despair?

Chapter 15

A day before the summer solstice, Hermes appeared to Charon.

"Zeus has asked me to take your place while you pay him a visit on Mount Olympus," the swift messenger of the king said. "You're to take his chariot. I've parked it next to Hades's."

It was common knowledge among the gods that chariot travel was much safer than god-travel. With the latter, an enemy could ambush the unsuspecting traveler and take him prisoner. But Charon didn't have any enemies—at least, none that he was aware of.

"Why the chariot?" Charon asked.

"My father thought you would enjoy the ride," Hermes said.

"Does my master know?"

Hermes boarded the skiff. "He does. Now off with you. The sooner you leave, the sooner you'll return and relieve me of this depressing post."

On Charon's way to the stables, the soul of the blind prophet, Tiresias, appeared, with his empty sockets and saggy breasts. In a menacing voice, he said, "Don't disturb our delicate balance."

Charon was taken aback. "Who, me? What are you talking about? I haven't disturbed anything. What have I done?"

"It's what you *will* do," the prophet said just before he disappeared.

Muttering his outrage to himself, Charon flew to the stables and found Zeus's chariot, parked beside Swift and Sure—the black stallions belonging to Hades. He stroked the manes of his old friends, hoping to calm his nerves. Why would Tiresias say such a thing? Charon was a devoted servant and had done nothing wrong. He didn't deserve a lecture, especially from the likes of Tiresias.

Still vexed from the encounter, Charon bid goodbye to Swift and Sure. Then he climbed into Zeus's chariot, took the reins of the four horses (which he'd always been told were the four great winds in the guise of horses), and drove from the chasm up into the sky to Mount Olympus.

As much as he hated to admit it, it was refreshing to be above ground again. He'd forgotten how lovely the sky was when there were few clouds and a gentle breeze. Maybe he had more in common with his sister, Hemera, and his brother, Aether, than he once believed.

Despite the beauty of his surroundings, Charon couldn't help but worry over Zeus's invitation. Why would the king of the Olympians wish to see him? After what had happened to Bill, Charon was wary of Zeus and his motives.

In fact, he hadn't forgiven Zeus. For centuries, Charon had admired the king for his mighty power and had thought of him as a mostly benevolent ruler and caretaker. But now, he despised Zeus and did not look forward to their meeting.

He was momentarily distracted from his heavy thoughts when Matilda prayed: *Johnny's video has over one million views! And that's without paying! It's gone viral, Charon? Do you know what that means? It's incredible! I think he's making a difference! I really do!*

Charon smiled at the good news as he pulled the chariot to the top of Mount Olympus. Outside the gates, he said, "Spring, Summer, Winter, Fall, open the gates, so that I, Charon, may enter."

A loud roar carried through the air as a tunnel of wind lifted, revealing a single rain cloud. After the wind settled and the rain diminished, the gates parted, and Charon drew the chariot forward, entering the gold-paved courtyard of Mount Olympus.

He passed a fountain with water shooting from the spout of a golden whale and headed for the stables, where he was greeted by Cupid, who tended the horses. From there, Charon flew back across the courtyard and up the rainbow steps to the main palace.

Inside, he passed the dining hall to his left and Hephaestus's forge to his right before entering the council room of thrones. Twelve thrones, one for each of the major Olympians, circled the perimeter of the room, and behind each throne was a door leading to the private chamber of each of the gods and goddesses. Above the council room was the great blue sky where the sun always shone.

Most of the thrones were unoccupied, as the gods spent much of their time away from Mount Olympus carrying out their various duties—at least, that's what Charon had come to believe, since the few times he'd visited, there hadn't been many at home.

Zeus and Hera were seated on their double throne at the back of the room. The other gods present were Hestia, Artemis, Demeter, Persephone, and Hecate.

"Look how beautiful you are!" Hera said.

The other goddesses gathered around and gaped at him in disbelief.

"So, Apollo was right!" Artemis pointed out. "You're cured?"

"I believe so," he said as he blushed with embarrassment from their attention.

Charon wondered if Persephone and Hecate had been made aware by Hades of what had transpired at the gates of the Underworld months ago, when Matilda had tried to resurrect her mother from the dead. If they did know, they didn't mention it. Instead, they asked him about his adventures in the Upperworld.

Although Zeus and Hera remained on their thrones as they listened to Charon's tales, the other goddesses present gathered around him as he gave a brief account of befriending Bill—leaving out the part about Zeus's offer and the fatal consequences to Charon's refusal. He also told them about Johnny and his bucket list—ziplining over the Amazon, smoking in Amsterdam, the 4-D experiences in Vegas, and the parade and festival in New Orleans. He skipped the part about stealing a car but shared, in great detail, the story of Etosha and M'Bari.

Artemis, the goddess of the wild, said she was pleased that the lions had been returned to their natural habitat.

Then, Hestia, the goddess of the hearth, put her lovely hand on Charon's shoulder. The gesture was unusual, since the Olympians typically showed disdain for the Underworld gods. "Aphrodite told me that you've fallen in love with a mortal named Matilda."

Charon clenched his fists, regretting that he'd ever asked the goddess of love and beauty for help. He should have known that she'd cause trouble for him.

"Is that true?" Persephone asked.

The ferryman couldn't prevent the blush from spreading through his cheeks again and giving his feelings away. "Yes, but we all know that nothing can come of it, so why speak of it, my lady?"

Hecate clicked her tongue. "We know nothing of the sort."

Charon raised his brows and studied Hecate's face, which was framed by the long and stunning streaks of white and black hair. Did she know something? Although she wasn't called upon as often as Apollo for her foresight, she did possess the talent. He prayed to her: *What do you see?*

Before she could reply, Zeus interrupted and said, "I'd like to share a private toast with Charon in my chambers, just the two of us, to celebrate his success."

Charon followed the king past the double throne and through the door made of solid gold. The ferryman's heart had never been more consumed by dread.

As he entered Zeus's private chambers for the first time in his long life, he found the painted murals, gilded molding, and jeweled sculptures and fabrics ostentatious. Golden eagles were painted across the ceilings and walls. A giant statue of a silver bull occupied one corner, and in the center of the main living area, surrounded by velvet chairs and couches, was a living oak tree growing through the ceiling. Perched on its branches were two pairs of finches, chirping in harmony.

A rustle higher up in the branches startled Charon, until he noticed it was Zeus's eagle.

"Don't let him frighten you," Zeus said dismissively. "He's just returned home from a secret mission and deserves a rest."

Charon wanted to say that he hadn't been frightened, but he held his tongue, though he wondered about the secret mission and why Zeus would mention it.

Zeus sat down at a golden table. "Come have a seat."

Charon joined him as Zeus poured them each a goblet full of ambrosia. "Let's toast to your good fortune."

Wary of a trap, Charon hesitated to put the cup to his lips.

"Come on, now, drink up. It's not poisoned. I'll even swear on the River Styx that it's not."

Charon lifted his brows. To swear an oath on the River Styx was a solemn vow that could never be broken. Anyone who dared break such an oath would be ripped apart by the Maenads—Dionysus's troupe of wild women drunk and immortal from potent wine.

He took a small sip of the heavenly brew.

"That's better," Zeus said.

Charon took a deep breath and wished this interview would end.

"Let me get straight to the point," Zeus said, as if he'd read the ferryman's mind. "I'm sure you know why you're here."

Charon had a suspicion, but he hoped he was wrong. "I'm sorry to say that I don't, my lord."

Zeus took a drink from his cup and stared haughtily at Charon. "Now, now. Don't pretend with me. You know what I want: the helm of invisibility."

The dread in Charon's heart tightened its grip. "I can't betray my master."

"I admire your loyalty. I really do. But there's something you've forgotten."

"What's that, Lord Zeus?"

"That *I* am you master. I am the master of *all*."

Charon took a deep breath but said nothing.

"If you obey me in this," Zeus continued, "I'm prepared to reward you."

"I need no reward for my obedience," Charon said, though he meant it as an impertinence.

Zeus gave him a smug grin. "I have a feeling you'll want to hear me out."

Charon clenched his jaw as the dread all but broke him.

"If you deliver the helm of invisibility to me, I swear on the River Styx to make your love—what is her name? Matilda?—immortal."

Charon fought the tears welling in his eyes as anger coursed through him. He should have known that Zeus would learn about Matilda and use her against him. He clenched his fists and asked, "And if I don't?"

"Well, you know what happened the last time you didn't do as I asked."

Tears slipped down Charon's cheeks as the impossibility of his situation became all too clear. The cost of Charon's refusal would mean Matilda's death.

In the old days, before his quest, the life of one mortal had meant nothing to him. In the general scheme of things, few gods made a fuss over the fortunes and misfortunes of a single man or woman. But Matilda was not just any woman—not anymore.

Through gritted teeth, he said, "I'll do it."

"That's a relief," Zeus said, climbing to his feet.

Charon stood to go and muttered, "Thanks for the drink."

"Take it with you. I insist. A loyal servant deserves such gifts. Expect many more."

Charon took the goblet of ambrosia and returned to the Underworld, to his abode. He set the goblet on his table and gazed at his reflection in the basin of water near his bed. He was still young and beautiful, but lines of worry and dread had marred his complexion. Such lines must be eternal, he thought.

* * *

Two days later, after Charon had dropped Thanatos and a soul from Japan at the deep healing pit of Erebus, he circled up the Phlegethon, past the Elysian Fields and the Dreamworld toward Tartarus, where all three Furies were carrying out their terrifying tasks of torture. They seemed to take great pleasure in their duties, as their lovely hair transformed into serpents and their beautiful eyes dripped with blood.

Tisiphone cried, "Murderer!" and lashed her victim with a whip, as her white wolf bared his teeth and growled.

"Rapist!" Meg knelt on the chest of her charge, a soul whose eyes had been plucked by Meg's falcon.

"Pedophile!" Alecto and her snake strangled a soul they had hanging upside down in midair.

Charon glanced at the iron gate that led to the seers' pit, deep down in Tartarus, where the Phlegethon did not flow. It was the only place in all of Hades that was shrouded in total darkness. Charon was tempted to look for Tiresias to ask him what he'd meant. Had he seen Charon stealing the helm and upsetting the delicate balance between the gods?

Meg sat up, noticing Charon's ferry had come to a stop. "Is there something you want?"

"I was just admiring your work," he said, as he tugged his pole through the river of fire. Then, he was struck with an idea. "And I was distracted by a silly thought. Please don't mind me."

"What silly thought?" Tisiphone wanted to know.

"Oh, it's nothing, really," Charon said. "Just something I got from my last passenger."

"Well, spit it out," Alecto insisted.

"He seemed to be under the impression that the helm of invisibility was guarded by Cerberus, when everyone here knows it's in a box beneath your father's throne. Silly, isn't it? What these mortals think of such things?"

"The joke's on you," Alecto said.

"Don't be rude," Meg warned her sister.

"What do you mean?" Charon baited Alecto.

"Our father keeps his helm on the table beside his bed," Tisiphone said. "So, you see? You don't know quite as much as you think."

"I'm put in my place, aren't I?" Charon laughed, as he continued on his way.

      * * *

At the next full moon, Charon left his boat and flew to the private bed chamber of Hades. The room was unoccupied, as he knew it would be. Hades preferred to stand guard at the gates with Cerberus, when the souls of the dead must wait a full day and night to be greeted by Charon and his skiff.

Charon wasn't surprised that the room wasn't warded against him. Why should it be? Hades trusted Charon and had no reason to believe he'd ever betray him. And, even now, if Hades were to enter the room, he would never suspect deception. Charon would only have to say that he'd been asked by Hecate to retrieve Persephone's favorite brush, and no more would need to be said.

The helm sat on the table, where the Furies had said it would be. There was nothing preventing Charon from picking it up and hiding it beneath his robes.

Tiresias's warning played over and over in his mind: *Don't disturb our delicate balance... It's what you will do.*

Would Charon upset the delicate balance between the gods by giving Zeus the helm?

The Fates, in their wisdom, had given each of the most powerful Olympians a single gift: Poseidon received the trident, Zeus the lightning bolt, and Hades the helm of invisibility. This way, one could not rise above the others and repeat the tyranny of their father, Cronos.

But if Zeus had the helm, would he become unstoppable?

At that moment, Matilda prayed to Charon about an internship she'd secured for the upcoming fall semester. She sang: *I'm a beast, I'm a beast, I'm on fleek, and I'm a beast!*

The contrast between Matilda's sweet chatter and his dark deed was jarring.

He imagined one of the Furies tormenting him in Tartarus and screaming, "Thief!"

And then he imagined his lord, Hades, and the look of disappointment that would cross his face.

Charon returned the helm of invisibility to its place and left the room.

* * *

The next few days were agonizing as Charon thought out every scenario that could come of his impossible situation. What good had it done for him to save Matilda from her near-fatal attempt at necromancy if she would die at Zeus's hand?

Troubled and desperate, Charon turned to his lord, Hades—his one and only true master.

Hades was pacing in his throne room when Charon stepped in the doorway.

"I'm sorry to disturb you, Lord Hades."

"What is it, Charon? Come inside, and tell me what's on your mind." Hades took a seat on his throne.

Charon approached, still not sure he was doing the right thing, but he'd gone this far, so he may as well keep going. "I need a favor, my lord."

"A favor?"

Charon feared that revealing Zeus's plan to Hades would backfire in ways that wouldn't be good for anyone, including himself. So, he'd come up with a plan of his own.

"I was hoping you'd allow me to return to the Upperworld for one more day."

Hades scratched at his beard. "May I ask why?"

"I have some unfinished business." He'd rather not go into detail, if he could avoid it.

"And you feel certain you can resolve this business in a single day?"

"I'm *not* certain of it, no, my lord." Charon sighed. "But I'd like to try."

"I doubt I can convince Hermes to take over again. We could ask Hecate."

"I'd like to go when I usually rest, during the next full moon, so we don't need to bother with replacing me at my post." Charon feared that Zeus would be suspicious if Hermes were called upon to take Charon's place.

"As long as you give me your word that you'll return before the day is over."

"I will, my lord. I promise."

"Very good, then, Charon. You may go."

Relief swept over him, though there was still much to do.

Chapter 16

Twenty-four days passed before the next full moon in mid-August, when Charon god-traveled from the Underworld to the hotel in Los Angeles to see Matilda. He had a funny feeling in the pit of his stomach as he stood in the hallway at her door. He'd replaced his robes with jeans and a button-down shirt, and now he thrust his hands into his pockets, trying to settle his nerves.

He knew she was home, because it was early morning, and she'd been praying to him as she'd readied for the first day of school for the fall semester.

He lifted his fist and rapped on the door.

"Just a minute!" came her sweet, sweet voice.

The anticipation felt like a bomb in Charon's chest, ready to explode. Centuries seemed to pass as he waited for Matilda to open the door.

Once she'd finally opened it, she gaped at him in utter shock. His heart seemed to leap from his chest as her face transformed from shock to bewilderment to joy.

She threw her arms around his neck. "Am I dreaming?"

He took her waist in his hands and lifted her in his arms. The feel of her body against him made him laugh with glee. "This isn't a dream. I'm really here."

"Come inside before I rip your clothes off in the hallway."

"The ward." He set her on her feet and pointed to the sigil above her doorway. "It won't let me pass."

"Hold on!" She ran inside her apartment and returned moments later with a pen. "Lift me up, so I can scratch it out."

With pleasure, he took her by the waist and flew up toward the ceiling.

She laughed hysterically as she kicked her legs like a swimmer. "I should have known you can fly. I suppose you can do just about anything!"

She rubbed the felt tip of her pen over the ward until it was a solid black square.

Hearing a group of mortals coming around the corner, Charon quickly god-traveled with Matilda into her room and closed the door behind them.

"What was that?" she said as they landed on their feet.

"God-travel. Now come and kiss me."

"I can't believe my eyes!" she cried. "You're here at last! It's a miracle!"

She grabbed his shirt and ripped it open, sending buttons flying in all directions. He laughed as she pressed her lips to his chest and made her way to his bellybutton.

She worked her way back up to his neck, caressing his skin with her lips. A moan escaped his throat as he reached for her blouse and lifted it over her head.

"Oh, Charon," she purred.

Her full breasts were cupped by a silky purple bra with delicate lace. He reached down and kissed the place where her breasts came together.

Matilda sighed and ran her fingers through his hair, grabbing fistfuls of it. She moved her hands to the base of his neck, and he lifted his face to meet hers.

When she plunged her tongue into his mouth, heat shot through his groin. He lifted Matilda into his arms and carried her to the bed.

"Please tell me you're here to stay," she whispered against his cheek as he lay beside her on the bed.

"I've found a way for us to be together," he said before he kissed the tip of her chin. "I want to make you immortal."

Matilda's eyes widened, and she sat up in the bed. "What?" She looked down at him, her curly hair cascading across her shoulders and concealing the breasts he longed to see.

He clasped his hands behind his head and sighed. He wished the mood hadn't changed. "It's not an easy process, so we need to discuss it first."

She sucked in her lips as he explained the process of apotheosis, which he had learned from Thanatos.

"You can't be serious," she said when he'd finished. "You want to set me on fire and trust that it will work?"

"I have a cup of ambrosia in my room." Ironically, it was given to him by the very god he hoped to thwart. "I was told by Thanatos that it would work."

"But won't it hurt like hell? What if I can't survive the pain?"

"Maybe you can give yourself a drug to make you sleep through the experience."

She shook her head. "No way. This is crazy talk. There must be another way. I'd rather bleed to death than be burned alive. Are you sure you can trust Thanatos? Maybe he has a thing against witches and wants me to burn."

"I know I can trust him. He's not the devious type."

She shuddered. "But burned alive? For real? Maybe I can find a spell..."

"We don't have time. I have to return to my post by the end of the day."

"The end of the day? Are you serious?"

He heaved a heavy sigh. "I wish I could say I wasn't."

"But I need time to think about this! Maybe I don't want to be a god. Would I still be able to be a doctor and help kids with cancer? Or will I have to live in the Underworld?"

"I don't know..."

She jumped up from the bed and paced the room. "Do I *want* to live forever?" She turned to him. "What if we get tired of one another?"

"I'd never get tired of you."

"You don't know that."

Charon frowned. It hadn't occurred to him that she might not want to be a god.

She gave him a half smile as she went to the bed and leaned down to kiss him. "I'm sorry, love. I don't mean to hurt your feelings."

"I want you to be honest."

"I want to be with you—I know *that*. I just don't know if I want to be a god. I've wanted to be a doctor for so very long. My work is important to me."

"I know it is."

"Can't you leave *your* job?" she asked. "Why should I have to give up *my* life? Can you leave the Underworld to live with *me*?"

"When you came for your mother, you wanted to stay with me," he pointed out.

"To give her back her life, yes," Matilda said. "You were a welcome consolation to giving up mine for hers. But that's impossible, right?"

He sighed. "Nothing's changed. You'd have to switch fates with her, and you wouldn't be the same. A

177

soul of the dead has no will and no memories—unless it's condemned to Tartarus, which wouldn't be the case with you."

"Then stay *here*, Charon!" she pleaded. "Stay here with me. Don't go back tonight."

"If a god abandons his duties, he'll eventually go insane."

"Oh." She chewed on her bottom lip. "But maybe there's a spell that can transform you into a mortal. Maybe it would stop you from going insane. Maybe we could live a nice, long, normal human life together. There's *got* to be a way."

He'd never considered giving up his post, much less his immortality. Even if there was a spell that could manage it and spare him from insanity, he doubted he could go through with it. And yet, here he was, asking her to give up what was important to her.

And none of this changed the fact that her life was now in danger of being destroyed by Zeus.

"But there's something you should know," he said.

She sat on the edge of the bed and looked down at him as he explained the new threat from Zeus.

"You're saying that the big chief of the gods wants to kill me if you don't do what he says?"

"Basically."

"Oh, shit." She stood up and crossed the room to the sliding glass doors that led to her balcony. As she gazed through the glass at the streets below, she said, "What are we going to do?"

He climbed from the bed and went to her, embracing her from behind. "If you don't want me to make you immortal..."

"I didn't say that." She held his hands where they rested against her bare stomach. "I just need more time to think about it."

He looked over her shoulder at the purple lace bra and the breasts peeking out of it. "Then we need to find a way to protect you."

"A protection spell..."

"I wonder if Hecate knows one strong enough to ward off Zeus."

She turned in his arms and reached up to kiss him. "Let's not think about any of this right now. Let's be together. After you go, we'll figure things out. Let's not waste any more time."

"You don't mind missing your first day of school?" he asked with a smile.

She smiled back at him, mischievously. "Come here, you."

* * *

At day's end, Charon reluctantly returned home to the Underworld after saying goodbye to his sweet Matilda.

As time passed, she kept him updated on her search for a protection spell strong enough to ward off Zeus.

I found a freeze protection spell, she prayed to him one day. *I've written this on a piece of paper: "I hereby bind Zeus, lord of the Olympians, from causing me harm, death, and destruction." Then I put the paper into a Ziplock freezer bag with water and froze it solid. I pray to Hecate that it holds!*

Not long after, she prayed: *I've drawn more protective wards around my door, and I've hidden some on the walls near my classrooms and the children's ward. Around my bed, I've placed candles at the four cardinal points with protective wards carved into each of them. I also bought crystals—onyx, emerald, ruby, and black tourmaline, and I wear them in my bra. I pray to Hecate that these things protect me from Zeus!*

Charon doubted such magic could affect a god. He'd been able to see though Matilda's glamour spell on Johnny, after all. But he was appreciative of her efforts and was anxious for Hecate to return to the Underworld. If anyone would know if the spells could ward off Zeus, it was the goddess of witchcraft.

One night, as Matilda lay in bed, she prayed: *I've been thinking about what it might be like to be a god. I wish I could know if I would be able to practice medicine and continue to work with children with cancer. If I knew I could do that, I might be more willing. Can you find this out for me?*

You must think I'm crazy for not jumping at the chance to be a god, like you. But it's not like trying to decide whether to buy a house or change careers or move to another city. This is a permanent change! I won't be able to go back! One minute, I think I would love to have power, to fly, and to do other godly things. And I think that, as a god, I might be able to do even more for children with cancer than I can do as a mortal. But I have so many unanswered questions, Charon. Help me, please!

Charon wasn't sure how he could ask the other gods questions without throwing suspicion his way. So far, he'd been able to count on Thanatos, so he sought his help again.

The next time Than boarded the skiff, Charon asked, "If I were to use the method you told me about—you know, the one your grandmother used for apotheosis..."

Than's brows shot up. "You're considering it, then?"

Charon directed his boat through the gates, up the River Styx, toward the Room of Judgment. "Don't tell anyone."

"You'll need to ask my father's permission."

"Of course," Charon said. "But nothing's been decided yet. Until then, mum's the word, got it?"

"Got it."

Charon stopped the ferry at the Room of Judgment. "Would Matilda be required to remain here with me in the Underworld, do you think? Or could she practice medicine up top?"

Than helped the soul from the boat before turning back to Charon. "The apotheosis won't stick if the new god doesn't find a purpose."

"A purpose?"

"A way to serve humanity or the world as part of the pantheon," he said. "I bring in the dead, you ferry them, Hip brings sleep, Athena brings wisdom...see where I'm going with this? Matilda would need to become the goddess of something, and, depending on that something, she would need to remain here or go up top to fulfill her duties."

"But she could sleep with me?"

Than gave him a wry grin. "Indeed."

Than led the soul to be sentenced by the three judges as Charon waited on the ferry.

As he waited, he received another update from Matilda: *I made a basil infusion with fresh basil leaves and boiling water. After my shower each morning, I use a cloth to soak my skin with the infusion. It's supposed to create a protective shield around me from any malevolent action. I pray to Hecate that it works!*

When Than and the soul returned to the boat with the verdict, Charon asked the god of death, "How would you feel about delivering another letter?"

"You forget how busy I am."

"You're to blame for this, Thanatos," Charon said. "You set us up, remember?"

"Fine. I'll deliver your letter."

Charon ferried Than and the soul to the Elysian Fields, where, as always, he stole glances at Bill and Johnny before continuing on his way.

* * *

In mid-September, at the next full moon, Charon drafted a letter to Matilda. He wrote:

My sweet Matilda,

Before my visit to the Upperworld, I never imagined I would feel this way about another living soul. As I carry out my duties, you are never far from my thoughts.

In a few moments, I hope to find you in your dreams and hold you in my arms for as long as you sleep. But first, I want to tell you what I learned in my quest for answers to your questions.

If you choose to go through the apotheosis, you must find a way to serve humanity or the world as part of the pantheon. You'll need to be the goddess of something—not of love or wisdom or family, because those are already taken. It must be something unique that you feel called to do.

Depending on your purpose, you may spend your time down here with me or in the Upperworld. Of course, when you need to sleep, you can share my bed, and then you can tell me in person where you like to be touched.

The good news is that the process need not be permanent. If you find you've made a mistake in becoming like me, simply fail to declare your purpose, and you will return to your mortal state.

As soon as Hecate returns from Mount Olympus with Lady Persephone, I'll ask her if she knows of a way that I can become mortal without losing my mind.

I'll see you in your dreams.

Charon

He folded the letter and left it on his table before he flew to the field of asphodel. He lay among the flowers and went to sleep, and then his psyche went in search of Matilda and her dreams.

Chapter 17

Charon wished he could remain with Matilda, kissing and flying and leaping on clouds, for much longer than the six hours they were together, but she woke up to her alarm to get ready for school, and so he returned to his abode and to the letter he'd written her. He tucked it into the folds of his robe and boarded his boat.

When he reached the gates, where he knew dozens of souls would be waiting with Than, he was surprised to find Hermes among them.

Hades, who'd been standing guard with Cerberus, gave a nod to Charon and returned to his chambers.

As Hermes boarded the boat with Than and the souls, he said, "My father sent me to ask you how you're coming along with the thing he asked you to do."

Charon arched a brow. "He told you?"

"No," Hermes said. "He said it didn't concern me, but he sent me for a progress report. Have you succeeded in whatever it is?"

"I'm working on it," Charon lied.

"Zeus is anxious for you to be done," Hermes said as they reached the Room of Judgment.

"Please tell him, with respect, that no one is more anxious than *I*," Charon said.

Hermes laughed. "I don't think I should. It'll put him off. I'll just say you're making progress." Then he added, "But he seems to think you should be finished by now, and you know how he can be."

"Yes. I do know." Charon frowned as the memory of Bill's death washed over him.

Hermes left, and Thanatos took the dozens of souls to be judged. Since there were many of them, this would take some time. Fortunately, Matilda's chatter was a welcome distraction. She reflected on her dream of him and how she would be thinking of it throughout the day. She also said that Johnny's video had reached two million views.

When Than returned with the verdicts for each soul, the god of death asked, "What was that about, with Hermes?"

Charon handed him the letter he'd written Matilda. "Don't ask."

Then Charon pulled his long pole through the Phlegethon and continued his rounds.

* * *

When Hecate and Persephone returned on the day of the fall equinox, Charon waited for an opportunity to speak to the goddess of witchcraft alone. There were many times, when he passed her on his boat, that his efforts were thwarted by the appearance of another— one of the Furies, Hip, or Than—all eager to welcome her home.

Meanwhile, Matilda had received his letter and had been praying to him about it: *I know I shouldn't be afraid to go through with it, but I am. It's a comfort to know I can change my mind and change back, but that doesn't make me feel better about being burned alive. I don't think I have the courage to endure it, Charon. I'm sorry. Can you find a way to come and live with me, as a mortal? We could both work with the children in the cancer ward. You can help them with their bucket lists while I try to cure them. We would be so amazing together!*

And if there's no way around the madness, can you find out how long before it would happen? Maybe you can live with me for the length of my mortal life and return to your duties before the madness sets in?

Many mortals get dementia in their old age. If that's what we can expect for you, rest assured that I would take care of you until my dying breath.

We have so much to think about. I'm eager to hear your thoughts.

It wasn't until the day after Hecate's arrival that he found the goddess, alone, swimming in the Acheron, just outside the gates where Cerberus stood guard.

On his way to meet Than and the souls waiting for him, Charon said to her, "I wonder if you might have a private word with me, by the Titan Pit, after I finish this round."

"What's it about?" she asked.

"I need some advice."

She narrowed her eyes at him. "We've lived here together for centuries, and you've never wanted my advice. What's changed, besides your appearance?"

"Will you meet me, or not?" he asked her, as Than and the souls approached him.

"I'll be there," she said, before she swam away.

"What was that about?" Than asked, once he'd boarded the skiff.

Charon shot him a look of annoyance.

"I know, I know," Than said. "Don't ask."

* * *

The Acheron made a loop around the borders of the Underworld. The Phlegethon made an inner loop, connected to the Acheron by the River Styx.

After the Room of Judgment, Charon steered his boat to the left if a soul was sentenced to Erebus or the Elysian Fields, and he went to the right if a soul was condemned to Tartarus. Either way, he would pass the Titan Pit at the furthest end of Tartarus, not far from the field of asphodel, on his way back around.

Hecate was waiting for him when he reached it. The place outside the Titan Pit was the best place for a private word, in Charon's opinion, because it was far away from everything but the Dreamworld, and everyone in the Dreamworld was fast asleep.

"Will you swear on the River Styx to tell no one of this conversation?" he asked Hecate as he approached.

"Why should I swear such a thing? Do you mean to do someone harm?"

"Quite the opposite. I'm trying to help one of your devoted followers."

Hecate put her hands on her slim hips and looked up at him with skepticism. "Which one?"

"Matilda Whitmore."

"Oh." Her eyes brightened with knowing. "So, this is the mortal that Aphrodite told us about. Your Matilda is also my Matilda. This explains a lot."

"What do you mean?"

"She thinks Zeus is after her. But why would he be?" She narrowed her eyes at him again and then lifted a brow. "Aha."

"Aha?"

"Zeus wants you to steal the helm of invisibility."

Charon felt the blood leave his face. "I won't do it. You must know that."

"I do; otherwise, Matilda wouldn't fear for her life."

"I thought I could save her by making her immortal. Demeter knows a way..."

Hecate nodded. "Where do you think she learned it?"

"Oh." Charon swallowed hard. He worried that his and Matilda's chances were ruined, since Hecate wasn't sworn to secrecy. But he'd gone too far to stop now. He had no choice but to trust her. "Well, Matilda is too afraid to go through with it."

"Who would blame her?"

"Not I, of course. But what else can we do to protect her?" Then he said, "The Underworld is guarded by wards that keep out Zeus and the other gods. Only Hermes is allowed in and out."

"Why are you telling me what I already know?"

"Could we mark Matilda with the same wards of protection?"

Hecate laughed. "They would protect her from rape, but not from being struck down by a lightning bolt. Even the Underworld isn't protected from that."

"Zeus swore to Hera that he wouldn't be unfaithful anymore," Charon pointed out. "He wouldn't dare..."

"I wouldn't be too sure about that," Hecate said. "But don't worry. Matilda is already warded against such things—not the lightning bolt, but the other."

Charon groaned. "There must be something we can do to protect her life."

"She could drink the wine of Dionysus."

"And become a Maenad?" Charon shuddered. "Absolutely not."

"Just until the danger blows over," Hecate pointed out. "The wine would protect her for as long as she drank it. Once the danger is gone, she could give up the wine and return to her normal life."

Charon clenched his jaw so hard that he had a new pain where the upper jaw met the lower, right beside his ears. "It sounds risky. How do we know she could give up the wine once she became drunk with it? Has any Maenad left her post once she's been recruited?"

"I don't know."

He sighed heavily. "Can you think of another way?"

"We could hide her."

"But she's in medical school."

"She could change schools—that's easy enough to manage. She could begin again, with a different name. Look how long Demeter stayed hidden after Hades married Persephone. It's easy enough to hide from Zeus, if you know how. Consider Prometheus..."

Charon mulled it over, suspecting it was the best option he'd heard so far.

"Ask me what you need to know," Hecate said, pulling him from his thoughts.

"Huh?"

"You want to know how you can become a mortal and abandon your duties without losing your mind."

He lifted his brows in surprise. "Do you know of a way?"

"I do, but it's horribly painful and risky, and you'll have to swear on the River Styx to tell no one about this method, whether you go through with it or not."

"I swear," he said.

* * *

At the next full moon, in mid-October, Charon waited anxiously for Hecate's arrival in his chambers. She'd promised to tell him the secret he'd sworn an oath to keep: how a god could abandon his duties, lose his immortality, and keep his mind.

As soon as she entered, she added new wards to the ones he'd already carved at the four cardinal points of his room.

"Just to be safe," she said.

He offered her a chair at his table, near the hearth where the Phlegethon flowed and cast light all around his dimly lit chamber. Then he poured her a glass of wine, given to him by Dionysus over a century ago for some favor—he couldn't now remember what.

As he sat across from her, she said, "I want you to swear again, on the River Styx. You'll repeat this to no one?"

"I swear."

She took a sip of the wine. "Many centuries ago, Circe the witch fell in love with a Titan whose name she never revealed to me."

"A Titan from the pit?"

"This was before the war."

Charon nodded. Then it was, indeed, a very long time ago.

Hecate continued: "The Titan didn't return her love, and she became bitter and resentful. She created this method. She swore to me that it worked, but I have no proof. Just her word."

"Why would she lie?" Charon asked.

"Pride. I don't want to mislead you into a false sense of confidence, Charon. I believed Circe was telling the truth, but there' no guarantee. That's why this is a risky and dangerous proposition. I'll leave it to you to decide if it's worth it."

"Go on, then. I'm listening."

"The god is first cut into pieces: first each limb and then the head."

Charon blanched. "Why not the head first, and spare him the rest of the pain?"

"Because the soul must endure the torment for this to work—at least, that's what Circe told me."

Nausea swept over Charon. He thought he might be sick, but he said, "Continue."

"The soul of the god must then possess a pig, by a spell of Circe's creation, to prevent Thanatos from taking it to Tartarus."

Although gods were immortal, when their bodies were decapitated or extremely maimed, their souls went to Tartarus while the body healed. The healing could take anywhere from a few hours to a couple of weeks, depending on the damage. As soon as the body was ready, it called the god's soul back from Tartarus, and the god was reborn.

But Circe had found a way to keep the soul from going to Tartarus by placing it into the body of a pig.

"Then what?" Charon asked.

"The dismembered body of the god is burned, and the ashes are spread across the seven seas with a special incantation."

Charon shuddered.

"The soul of the god is released from the pig and forced to walk the earth for forty days and forty nights," she said.

Charon's jaw dropped. "As a ghost? An untethered spectral?"

Hecate nodded. "That's the length of time required for the ashes of the body to find themselves again and reform."

"A god's body will reform, even after all that?"

"Indeed. And once it's ready to call for its soul, the body is placed in the center of a pentagram with candles at each point. An incantation is uttered as the soul rejoins the body."

"Is that the end? Or is there more?"

"That's the end of it."

"Thank the gods."

"It's no trifle, that's for sure," she said. "Any god who wishes to undertake this process must first think long and hard."

"Is it reversible?"

"I don't know."

Charon scratched his chin for a few moments, pondering what he'd heard. Then he asked, "If I choose to go through with it, would you help me?"

"Only if Matilda asks it of me," she said. "I'd need to be sure that she wants it as badly as you."

He'd hoped to spare Matilda the details of his pain and agony, but he supposed he should be grateful for Hecate's help, even with her conditions.

"Thank you," he said. "I'll let you know what I decide."

* * *

After Hecate had left, and before the full moon had ended, Charon god-traveled to the field of asphodel to seek Matilda in her dreams. He hoped he wasn't too late. If she hadn't already awakened, she would be doing so soon.

He found her standing on a rope between two trees beneath raging rain and winds.

He flew to her and asked, "What are you doing here?"

"Apparently, this is my new home," she said. "Can you believe it? I feel like I'm going to fall at any moment."

"Your new home?" He laughed. "Matilda, you're dreaming. This isn't really your home."

She blinked and looked up at him as she struggled to maintain her balance. "It doesn't matter. My home is wherever you are."

He lifted her into his arms and commanded the rain and wind to cease. Then he turned the setting into a sandy beach beneath the warm rays of Helios and a wide blue sky.

"Let's sit together," he said. "We need to talk."

He carried her to the sand, and they sat side by side facing the sparkling, gentle waves. "Hecate said there *is* a way for a god to become a mortal without going mad."

"This really is a dream, then. I don't believe it."

"It's not an easy process." He took a deep breath. "And you must swear on the River Styx to tell no one."

"Who would I tell?"

"Athena. She can't know. No one can."

"I swear."

He told her all about it, as he'd been told by Hecate.

"No way," she said. "Uh-uh. I'm not letting you go through that. I'd rather be burned alive."

"I'd do it all for you," he said in between kissing her. "Whatever it takes."

She pressed her body against his and grabbed fistfuls of his hair. "I love you, Charon. I love you so much."

Tears threatened to slip from the corners of his eyes. He forced them back and whispered, "I love you, too."

Chapter 18

For two weeks, Charon wrestled with the choice given to him by Hecate, when, on Halloween night, exactly one year from the day he was first sent to the Upperworld for his quest, Charon went in search of the goddess with his decision.

The last soul on board had just been dropped off with Than in the Elysian Fields. Charon was making the return trip toward the gates, when he passed the Titan Pit, where he had first enlisted Hecate's help. Seeing the ominous iron door of the pit made him realize that immortality without Matilda would be the worst punishment he could endure. He was only prolonging his suffering by putting off the inevitable. He had to go through with Circe's method if he was ever to find happiness again.

He summoned Hecate to his boat.

She appeared, floating above the Phlegethon. "You called?"

"I'll do it."

"I need to hear it from Matilda."

"You will. Be ready at the next full moon."

She frowned but said nothing before she disappeared.

With very little time before his next round, Charon scribbled out a letter imploring Matilda to pray to Hecate.

He wrote:

My sweet Matilda,

It's better that I, a god, should accept the price of our togetherness than you, a mortal, because I am inherently stronger and more durable than you. Trust me that I will not feel nearly as much pain in the process to unmake my immortality as you would in the one to make yours.

If you love me, ask Hecate to change me, so that we can be together for the rest of our mortal lives.

Yours Forever,

Charon

When he reached the gate, he handed the letter to Than. "This is the very last time I shall ask this of you, my friend."

Thanatos took the letter and gave Charon a solemn nod. He knew better than to ask questions, as they continued toward the Room of Judgment.

    * * *

At the next full moon in early November, Charon lay stretched out on an altar, prepared by Hecate, in the privacy of his chambers. Candles were lit at the four cardinal points. Sage burned on a table near the door. A line of salt encased them in a circle around the altar, where a pig, squealing its outrage, was chained.

Hecate held an ax. "Are you sure of this?"

The memory of Matilda reading his fortune with the tarot cards suddenly came to him, and he wondered if this is what the cards had foreseen. It was hard to believe it had been a year ago. Johnny had still been alive, and Charon had barely begun his adventures.

"Charon?" Hecate brought him from his reverie.

He clenched his jaw to keep his teeth from chattering. "Do it."

She brought the ax down hard against his right arm, just at the shoulder, but failed to make a clean break. Surprisingly, he felt little pain...at first.

When she brought the ax down again, and he witnessed his arm fall to the floor and the blood spurt from the empty socket of his shoulder, a sharp and burning pain consumed the entire right side of his body, and he screamed in agony.

He used every bit of willpower he possessed to avoid begging Hypnos to put him into the deep boon of sleep.

No one could know.

Hecate lifted the ax and brought it down on the left side.

Dizzy and nauseous, Charon's body began to flail of its own accord. Hecate struggled against him, tightening the ropes around his ankles.

"Do you want to stop?" she asked.

He shook his head. Barely able to breathe, he muttered, "Keep going."

Frowning and in tears, Hecate lifted the ax and brought it down to cleanly sever the left arm. Charon heard it fall to the floor as blood spurted into his face and mouth and choked him.

He coughed and wildly flailed his head, the pain unbearable.

"Let's stop this craziness," Hecate pleaded. "Haven't you had enough?"

Charon felt as if he were losing consciousness. The face of Hecate shimmered, and suddenly it was Tiresias looking down at him.

"Don't disrupt our delicate balance," the blind prophet said.

"But I haven't," Charon muttered. "I didn't take the helm."

"What?" Hecate's face reappeared. "I know you didn't."

Her face shimmered, and again, it was Tiresias looking down at him.

"By abandoning your duties, you disrupt the pantheon," the old prophet warned. "Hades will fall."

"Tiresias?" Charon asked as he closed his eyes and tried to regain focus.

"Charon, it's *me*. It's Hecate. What are you talking about?"

He opened his eyes to see Hecate staring down at him with a face full of tears and dread.

"This was a mistake," she said. "Let's end this. Let's stop this. Please?"

Disturbed by his vision of Tiresias, Charon relented with a weak nod.

* * *

Hours later, after Charon's body had healed from its dismemberment and Hecate, with swollen eyes and trembling hands, had left him, he flew to the field of asphodel to tell Matilda about his change of heart.

Once again, he found her precariously perched on a rope between two trees beneath raging winds and falling rain.

"This again?" he asked as he took her in his arms.

"It's my new home," she said. "Can you believe it? How am I supposed to live like this?"

"You're dreaming, my love," he said before he kissed her.

Then he changed the setting to a field of flowers beneath the shining rays of Helios. A roaring waterfall could be heard and seen in the distance, surrounded by colorful hills and foliage.

He lay her in the field of flowers and stretched out beside her. Propped up on an elbow, he gazed down at her beautiful face.

"I have something to tell you," he said.

Once he'd told her of his change of heart, including the warning from Tiresias, she buried her face in his neck and wept.

"It kills me that you endured so much for nothing," she said. "But it makes me crazy happy to know how much you love me—the lengths you'd go to be with me."

"I'm sorry I didn't go through it."

"We don't want to be the cause of Hades's downfall, however badly we want to be together."

He kissed her again and stroked her cheek.

"Have you ever thought of talking to him?" she asked.

"Who? Hades?"

She nodded. "Maybe he could offer us some advice."

"I'd hate for him to know that I almost abandoned him," Charon admitted. "But maybe he'll respect the fact that, in the end, I didn't."

She smiled up at him. "Now I have hope again."

He smiled and kissed her sweet face, but he had less hope than he let on. What could Hades say to change this impossible situation?

* * *

The following morning, when Charon returned to the gates where Cerberus and Hades had been standing guard, Charon hailed his lord before meeting Than and the waiting souls.

"You wish to speak to me?" Hades asked as the skiff neared.

"Yes, my lord," Charon said. "May I come to your throne room after I finish my first round?"

"I suppose it can't wait?"

"It can. I'm at your disposal."

Hades pulled at his beard. "On second thought, come as soon as you can. I'll be waiting for you."

Charon bowed his head, "Thank you, my lord."

Charon dragged his pole through the Acheron, where Than and the souls boarded, before heading back up the Styx and through the gates to the Room of Judgment.

Once he'd dropped everyone at their respective destinations and he was alone on the skiff, he docked the boat at the great palace and flew to meet his master.

Hades was sitting on his throne with one leg crossed over the other, and, as was his usual habit, he was pulling at his beard.

"Oh, there you are, Charon," he said when he saw the ferryman in the doorway. "Come in and tell me what's on your mind."

As Charon began his story of Matilda, Hades interrupted, "Yes, Persephone told me all about it, from what she heard during your visit to Mount Olympus."

"I love her, my lord," Charon said, trying to hide the desperation in his voice. "We want to be together."

"Perhaps Zeus would..."

Charon shook his head. "He wouldn't."

"Have you already asked? How do you know?"

"I'd prefer not to say." Charon averted his eyes.

"Oh," Hades stood up and paced in front of his throne. "He wants you to steal my helm."

The blood drained from Charon's cheeks as his jaw dropped open. "How do you know?"

"He's always trying to steal it. That's nothing new."

Charon cupped his chin, trying to take that in. "He threatened to kill Matilda. I was afraid it would start a war if I told you. I nearly abandoned my duties to be with her."

Hades stopped his pacing. "Nearly?"

"I couldn't do it."

Hades crossed the room to stand before Charon. Now that the ferryman was no longer bowed and ravaged by old age, they were equal in height and build.

The lord of the Underworld clapped his hands onto Charon's shoulders. "I appreciate your loyalty, Charon. I really do." He released him. "And I'll do everything in my power to protect Matilda."

"Thank you, my lord. At least that offers me some comfort."

Hades crossed his arms. "What if I allowed you to go to her at every full moon? Could you live with that?"

"If there were no other choice—though her lifetime wouldn't be nearly long enough, if I'm to go on without her."

"I see."

"I'd considered blackmailing Zeus," Charon said suddenly. "I was going to threaten to expose what he'd asked me to do, hoping the fear of being despised by the other gods would force him to turn Matilda into one of us."

Hades returned to his throne and pulled at his beard. "I'm afraid that alone wouldn't be enough to secure his cooperation."

Charon sighed and dropped his head, allowing the desperation and despair to overwhelm him.

"But maybe you can sweeten the deal to make it irresistible," Hades added.

Charon lifted his head. "How, my lord?"

Hades smiled. "Threaten to expose him to *Hera*."

"Expose him?"

"You recall that some years ago, he swore an oath to never cheat on her again."

"I do recall."

"You and I both know how impossible it is for Zeus to keep such promises."

"But without proof..."

"So, find it," Hades challenged. "The proof is out there, somewhere. Find it and use it against him."

Charon had no idea where to begin.

Hades crossed one leg over the other and leaned back in his chair. "If you can threaten him with both—to turn the gods *and* his wife against him—then you will have the king of the Olympians eating out of your hand."

* * *

At the next full moon, ten days before the winter solstice, Charon flew to Tartarus, to the seers' pit, where the Phlegethon did not flow, to confront Tiresias. If anyone might shed some light on how Charon could collect evidence against Zeus, he believed the blind prophet could.

Charon descended into the depths of the pit and called out, but he found no one at home. He'd forgotten that the seer wandered all of Hades these days and even spent time among the Elysian Fields.

He was about to leave when Tiresias appeared at the gate to the pit.

"I see you," Tiresias said. "What do you want from me?"

"Obviously, I didn't go through with it," Charon said.

"Go through with what?"

"Circe's method. Your warning put a stop to it."

"I have no idea what you're talking about. Are you speaking in riddles?"

Charon crossed his arms and sighed. "You came to my chambers last month, when Hecate was performing..."

"I've never been to your chambers, Charon, ferryman of the dead. Why are you in mine?"

Charon bit his tongue. Why would the seer lie? "I don't wish to disrupt our delicate balance."

"But you'll do it anyway," Tiresias said. "No one ever listens to me. It's my curse."

Anger rose in Charon's throat. "I refused to steal the helm. I refused to abandon my duties. What more can I do?"

"Leave me alone, for starters," the old prophet said as he flew past and began to descend into the darkness.

"Wait," Charon called. He cut his wrist with the dagger he carried in his boot. He knew a soul of the dead could never resist the smell and taste of blood.

Tiresias returned and drank the blood from Charon's wrist.

As the old prophet drank, Charon asked, "I need evidence that Zeus has been unfaithful to Hera in recent years. Do you know where I can find it?"

Tiresias continued to drink until Charon pulled his arm away.

"Answer me, and I'll give you more," Charon demanded.

"I had a vision last year of Zeus raping a girl from a small village in Greece," Tiresias said. "I don't know which village. I don't know the girl's name."

"Could you swear to this before Hera?" Charon asked.

"She won't believe me. People rarely do."

Charon groaned. "That's not much help, then, is it?"

"The girl became pregnant, as they always do," Tiresias continued. "When the child was born, the girl murdered it."

"A sad story, but not what I need."

"The girl died recently of pneumonia and was sentenced to Tartarus," Tiresias said.

Charon's brows lifted. "She's in Tartarus? Can you describe her?"

"I saw short black hair and blue eyes. She wore a polka-dotted scarf on her head. Her child's in Erebus, and she longs for it. That's all I know."

Tiresias grabbed Charon's wrist and continued to drink.

Charon let him drink for as long as he wished. The old prophet deserved it. For the first time in many months, the ferryman felt hopeful again. If he could find the soul of Zeus's victim, he might be able to force the king's hand to turn Matilda into one of them.

Chapter 19

Charon left the seers' pit and flew to the main region of Tartarus, where the Furies were busy inflicting punishment on three of their charges.

"What do *you* want?" Alecto demanded as her snake hissed from around her neck.

"Don't be rude," Meg warned her sister. Then, stroking the feathers on her falcon, she turned to Charon. "But really, what *do* you want?"

"I'm looking for someone," he said.

"Could you be more specific?" Tisiphone said from where she stood with her whip. Her wolf howled as she brought the whip down on the back of a tethered soul.

"I don't know her name," Charon admitted.

"Good luck with that." Alecto turned to the soul she had strapped to a table and continued her work.

To Meg, Charon said, "She killed her newborn baby."

"We have a lot of those," Meg said. "Do you know anything more?"

"She's from a village in Greece. She wore a polka-dotted scarf on her head."

Since the apparitions of souls took the form of their most recent living appearance, there was a chance the detail of the scarf would make a difference.

"Anything else?" Meg asked.

"Her child is still in Erebus. I'm told she longs for it."

"That's true of most of them," Meg said. "I'm afraid you'll have to search for yourself."

Charon followed the Fury past the tools of torment to the back of Tartarus, toward the Hydra's sinkhole, where thousands of forlorn souls sat, paced, or stood as they endured their boredom and suffering.

He walked among them, asking if any had been attacked by Zeus within the last year. He cut himself and fed hoards of them but found no answers.

Meanwhile, Matilda's prayers to him had grown less hopeful and were once again tinged with despair: *Are we not meant to be? Are the Fates against us?*

She performed tarot readings almost daily and shared what they foretold: *You'll have to make a very difficult decision in the coming days.*

Like he didn't already know that, he thought bitterly.

Once, she alarmed him by praying: *Sometimes I wonder if this is all in my head. Am I overstressed with work and school? Maybe I'm delusional in thinking that I've met a god and fallen in love with him. Maybe you don't even exist.*

Every day, at mid-day, he took a break from his rounds to search the miles and miles that stretched across the region of Tartarus. He wouldn't give up, no matter how badly the odds were stacked against him.

One day in February, he spotted a small and frail-looking thing with short black hair and blue eyes. She paced among others, but what made her stand out to Charon was the polka-dotted scarf tied around her waist.

"Have you seen my baby girl?" she asked him.

"Yes," he said, answering truthfully, for he saw every soul that entered Hades, even if he couldn't remember them all.

Meg noticed him, and she flew over to ask what he was doing.

"Looking for answers," he said.

Charon took his dagger and slit through the palm of his hand and offered it to the soul.

The soul of the dead lapped up his blood eagerly before he pulled it away.

"Who was the father of your baby?" Charon asked.

"No one ever believes me when I say."

"Tell me. I'll believe you."

"Zeus. My baby's father was Zeus."

Meg shot him a look of surprise. "What are you up to?"

"Don't be rude," he said with a smile. "This is no concern of yours."

Meg pouted and left with a huff.

Charon asked the soul of the dead for her name, for the name of her village, and for the date of her child's birth. Then he gave her more of his blood as he plotted his next move.

* * *

At the spring equinox, after Persephone and Hecate had left for Mount Olympus, Charon summoned Hermes to his chambers.

Hermes appeared in the doorway and found himself unable to enter. Charon had forgotten that the wards carved by Hecate excluded everyone, including the swift messenger god of Zeus.

"Forgive me, Hermes," Charon said as he scratched away the wards. "Come inside, please, and have a seat."

"I don't have time to stay."

"That's just as well," Charon said. "Would you please tell you father that I have what he's been asking for?"

Charon didn't feel guilty for the deception, because he spoke the truth. Zeus *was* going to get what he was asking for, in a manner of speaking.

Hermes grinned and clapped his hands. "Great news. He'll be in a good mood after I tell him."

"One more thing," Charon said. "I need to arrange a meeting with him. He'll know why."

"I'll return with a date and time, and I'll send the chariot, to boot."

Charon shook his head. "Your father will need to meet me here, in secret."

"In your chambers?"

"That wouldn't be wise," Charon said. "The seers' pit, I think. I'll arrange for it. Tell him to come tonight, before the full moon begins to wane."

"Will do," Hermes said before he disappeared.

A few moments later, Hermes reappeared. "For some reason, my father suspects a trap."

"Tell him I swear on the river Styx that I do not intend to trap him," Charon reassured him.

Hermes quickly disappeared.

A moment later, he returned. "Zeus will meet you in the seers' pit at midnight, Greek time."

Charon smiled. "Very well. Thank you, Hermes."

When the messenger god left, Charon flew to the field of asphodel, to seek out Matilda in her dreams. He wouldn't risk revealing his plan, where Hypnos might overhear. But he wanted to reassure her that he wasn't a figment. He needed her to know that she hadn't imagined him. He doubted her dream was the place to convince her, but until he had another option, he would do what he could to make her believe in him again.

* * *

Just before midnight, Charon waited for Zeus in the seers' pit, where even Tiresias was not to be found. As the ferryman waited, he suddenly felt foolish for not asking for help from Thanatos, or Hades, or one of the Furies. Even Hecate might have been summoned from Mount Olympus to aid him. It would have been wise to have brought an ally. What if Zeus, after hearing what Charon had to say, swallowed the ferryman whole—or, worse, struck him down with a lightning bolt and threw him into the Titan Pit?

Zeus was late, and Charon began to fear he wasn't coming. Perhaps it was best. The ferryman would have a chance to bring a friend at the next meeting.

As Charon was about to fly away, the king of the Olympians appeared and said, "Do you have the helm?"

"I'd like a word, my lord." Charon struggled to keep the fear from his voice.

"I don't have time for this. Do you have the helm or not?"

"I think you'll want to hear what I have to say. It concerns a girl you raped about a year ago. Her name was Agatha Galanos."

"What is the meaning of this impertinence?" Zeus demanded as his face grew red with rage.

"I want to offer you a deal."

"How dare you? I don't need to hear this from the likes of you." Zeus disappeared.

"I'll tell Hera!" Charon shouted. "You broke your oath!"

Zeus returned, his face so red that Charon thought the king would explode. "You broke *your* oath. You told Hermes this wasn't a trap."

"It isn't, my lord. You're free to come and go."

"And what's to prevent me from smiting you down in your boots and paralyzing you for all eternity?"

Charon told himself to remain calm. He clasped his hands, to keep them from trembling. "Hades knows you tried to use me for the helm. What will he do without his ferryman? And who would take my place? *Hermes*?" Charon forced a laugh. "Hades will blame you. Do you want to start a war?"

"Maybe I'll take my chances," Zeus growled.

"If I disappear, I have a friend who'll tell your secret." Charon was thinking of Meg. The Fury had overheard Charon's conversation with Agatha Galanos.

Zeus flew close to Charon and glared at him, his face inches from the ferryman's face. "What do you want from me?"

Charon took a deep breath. "I want you to turn Matilda Whitmore into one of us. Make her immortal."

The king of the Olympians flew across the room and pounded his fist on Charon's table, cracking it in half. "Am I to understand that not only are you *not* giving me the helm, but you're attempting to coerce me into making someone immortal?"

"That's the gist of it, my lord." Charon stifled a smile that threatened to spread across his trembling lips. "If you don't want everyone to know you broke your oath to Hera and threatened me to get the helm."

"This is extortion!"

"Indeed, it is."

Zeus groaned. "I need time to think. I'll leave you now."

"So you can further plot against me?" Charon said. "I don't think so, my lord. If you leave this pit without swearing an oath to me on the River Styx, I'll tell your secrets. I promise you that."

Zeus grabbed the goblet of ambrosia he'd once given to Charon and flung it across the room.

Charon tried another approach. "I know you love Hera, my lord, despite your transgressions. And she loves you."

Zeus narrowed his eyes at the ferryman. "What are you getting at?"

"I want to have love in my life, too, don't you see? Make Matilda a goddess, and our problems are solved."

"*Your* problems, perhaps, but not *mine*."

Charon sighed. Maybe this wasn't going to work after all.

Zeus sat down in one of Charon's chairs by the broken table. "If I do this for you, there will be consequences. First and foremost, it will set a precedence. How many other gods who fall in love with mortals will want the same? New gods will upset our delicate balance."

A chill snaked down Charon's spine. Upset the delicate balance? Those were the words of Tiresias.

Feeling desperate now that his plan was doomed to fail, Charon said, "No one needs to know."

Zeus cocked a brow and leaned forward. "What do you have in mind?"

"Matilda wants to practice medicine and help children with cancer," Charon began. "There's no need for her to officially join the pantheon, to ever go to Mount Olympus, or to be known by the other gods. We can keep her immortality a secret."

"But the Underworld gods will know, and word is sure to spread."

"We could get them to swear..."

Zeus stood up. "No. It's too risky. The more people we involve, the worse the situation becomes. We have to minimize the damage as much as possible."

"You were willing to make her a goddess when you wanted the helm," Charon pointed out.

"Because in having the helm, there would have been no reason to keep the delicate balance between us in place. I would have had the upper hand in all things. Now, the situation is different."

Charon was on the verge of panic. His plan was failing, and he was all but doomed. He wracked his brain for some way out of this desperate situation, but came up short. Was there nothing he could do?

He was about to offer to steal the helm when Zeus said, "I have an idea, but you won't like it."

Charon took a deep breath. "What is it, my lord?"

"She mustn't ever come here—not to the Underworld, not to Mount Olympus, not to anyplace sacred to the gods."

"What?"

"You will see her at each full moon, when you rest from your duties, but you must go to *her*. She can't come here."

"And she will be immortal?"

"You must agree to swear to abide by my conditions, and one thing more."

Charon was overwhelmed with emotions—hope, despair, joy, sorrow. "What, my lord?"

"Since Hades, and perhaps others, already know that I attempted to coerce you into stealing the helm, I want them to believe you were punished for not following through with it."

"Punished? What do you mean?"

"I want to take away your youth."

Charon's mouth fell open as tears filled his eyes. "You want to do what?"

"You heard me."

"But, my lord..."

"If you want me to make Matilda immortal, you must agree..."

"But how will she love me in that state?"

Zeus crossed his arms and then used one hand to cup his chin. He seemed to be thinking. Meanwhile, Charon was trying to process what had just transpired between them. He was so confused with overwhelming emotions, he wasn't sure what to think. Would he really lose his youth?

"I have an idea," Zeus finally said. "I'll fix so that Matilda will see you as you are now. But to everyone else, you'll be as you *were*, before your quest. And that is my final offer, Charon. Take it or leave it."

Charon didn't care how he looked to everyone else; it only mattered that he was beautiful for Matilda. And, truly, the full moon would have been their only time together, even if she'd been allowed to live with him and to commune with the other gods.

"Well?" Zeus demanded. What do you say?"

"I'll take it," Charon said.

"Very good," Zeus said. "Let's both swear to our agreement and get on with it."

Chapter 20

The next day, each Underworld god to lay eyes on Charon gawked at his aged and decrepit state and asked, "What happened to you?"

"I was punished by Zeus for refusing to steal the helm," he said to each of them.

He was touched by their pity and wished he could reveal his secret, but he kept his oath to Zeus. No one must know the truth.

Thanatos was especially kind when they first met on the boat. The god of death felt he was to blame for the ferryman's troubles.

"At least I'm not dying anymore," Charon told him. "It's an improvement to how things were."

"What of Matilda?" Than asked.

"I'll visit her until her final days."

"Will she accept you as you are?"

"She's a witch, remember? She can use a glamour spell to make me more...palatable."

"I see."

* * *

Later that day, Hades summoned the ferryman to his palace.

When Charon appeared in the doorway of the throne room, his lord said, "I'm sorry that this was your reward for your loyalty to me. I can't make it up to you, I realize, but perhaps there's something I can do."

Charon lingered in the doorway. "It's not necessary, my lord."

Hades was sitting on his throne, and now he crossed one leg over the other. "Even so, I want you to take the new moon, too."

Charon crossed the room to stand before his lord. "What?"

"You could visit your sweetheart twice a month, for as long as she lives. Wouldn't you like that?"

"You want me to take the new moon *and* the full moon?" Charon could barely contain his excitement.

"It's not nearly enough to thank you for what you've endured for me and for my kingdom."

"Thank you, Lord Hades."

Hades stood and grabbed Charon's shoulders. Now that Charon's back was bowed with old age and his bones were thin and frail again, he was no longer as tall or as broad as the lord of the Underworld.

"Thank you, Charon, for your loyalty. I want you to know how much I value your service."

"It's my pleasure, my lord."

* * *

In early April, Charon and Matilda lay side by side in Matilda's bed after a night of lovemaking. It felt good to Charon to have his youth, beauty, and vitality restored while he was in the arms of his beloved. It felt good to hold her, to ache for her, and to never want to leave her side.

"What a pleasure it is to have you in my bed," Matilda said. "Are you sure this isn't a dream?"

He laughed and kissed her again. "It does feel like a dream, even to me."

"It will feel even more like one when you teach me to fly."

"I told you, we can't draw attention to ourselves."

She grinned. "I'll convince you yet. You just wait."

"There is something on my mind, though," he said somberly. "Not flying. Something else."

"What is it?" she asked, leaning over him.

Her long curls cascaded over her shoulders and swept against his bare chest.

"Are you sure you're okay with not having children? We can keep *your* immortality a secret, but to bring a child into the world, an immortal being..."

"I have enough children in my life," she said before she kissed his cheek. "The cancer kids are my children. I'm devoted to them. You know that."

"You never wanted any of your own?"

"I don't know. I don't think so. Anyway, it no longer matters. Just know I couldn't be happier."

"I think you could. You once said you wanted a normal mortal life. What will people think when years go by, and you still look the same?"

"Remember the glamour spell I used on Johnny?"

"How will that help?"

"I can live here for sixty years or so before I'll have to move."

He propped himself up on an elbow and stroked her hair. "You won't mind moving?"

"Just think: I can help fight children's cancer all over the world, until it's completely abolished! If you don't think that makes me the happiest girl in the world, then you don't know me!"

He laughed with glee. "And what will you do when you've abolished all forms of cancer?"

"Move on to the next disease. And the next. And the next."

He lay beside her again and held her in his arms. "I'll follow you wherever you go, for however long you'll have me."

"Then plan to follow me forever, my love," Matilda said before she kissed the ferryman once more.

The End

* * *

Charon's Quest is a stand-alone novel that shares the world of Eva Pohler's bestselling series, *The Underworld Saga*. To read more about one of the most beloved pantheons in human history, visit Eva's website. The first book in the series, *Thanatos*, is "sure to thrill"—*Kirkus Reviews*.

www.evapohler.com
* * *

If you'd like to receive news about Eva's upcoming releases and giveaways, subscribe to Eva's newsletter and receive a free ebook copy of *Vampire Addiction*.

"Great first book in the series! Loved the connection between vampires and Greek mythology. Can't wait to see what happens next!" –Michelle Madow, author of *The Elementals Series*

Visit Eva's website to subscribe!

Made in the USA
Middletown, DE
01 August 2020

14212979R00124